PENGUIN BOOKS

FEI
and Other

KU-134-955

The trouble with Mick Collier is that he doesn't care where he puts his feet; kicking a rival in the ankle or treading roughly on Jane's feelings – it's all the same to him.

This story of a school tennis star who eventually trips up on his own casual tactics is just one of eight poignant and realistic stories from one of today's leading storytellers. With a perfect ear for dialogue and a sharp eye for detail, Jan Mark shrewdly observes the pangs of heartache and the love–hate relationship with parents – two themes which are bound to strike a chord with all teenage readers.

'Jan Mark is brilliantly good at catching the tones of voice of today's young, and wickedly good at catching those of our teachers' – *The Times Educational Supplement*

Jan Mark grew up in Kent and attended the Canterbury College of Art; afterwards she went on to teach art at Gravesend. She started her writing career in 1973, and since then has written a large number of highly successful books, for which she has been awarded the Carnegie Medal and other prestigious prizes. Everything she does now is connected with books and writing, and she has spent two years as writer-in-residence at Oxford Polytechnic. She lives in Oxford.

Jan Mark

FEET

AND OTHER STORIES

illustrated by
BERT KITCHEN

PENGUIN BOOKS

PENGUIN BOOKS

Published by the Penguin Group
Penguin Books Ltd, 27 Wrights Lane, London W8 5TZ, England
Penguin Books USA Inc., 375 Hudson Street, New York, New York 10014, USA
Penguin Books Australia Ltd, Ringwood, Victoria, Australia
Penguin Books Canada Ltd, 10 Alcorn Avenue, Toronto, Ontario, Canada M4V 3B2
Penguin Books (NZ) Ltd, 182–190 Wairau Road, Auckland 10, New Zealand

Penguin Books Ltd, Registered Offices: Harmondsworth, Middlesex, England

First published in Kestrel Books 1983
Published in Puffin Books 1984
Reprinted in Penguin Books 1991
7 9 10 8 6

Copyright © Jan Mark, 1978, 1980, 1983
Illustrations copyright © Bert Kitchen, 1983
All rights reserved

'Feet' first appeared in *Love You, Hate You, Just Don't Know* (Evans Brothers, 1980); 'Poor Darling' first appeared in *You Can't Keep Out the Darkness* (The Bodley Head, 1980); 'I Was Adored Once Too' first appeared in *Is Anyone There?* (Puffin, 1978); 'Still Life: Remote Control' first appeared in *Young Winter's Tales* (Macmillan, 1978)

Printed in England by Clays Ltd, St Ives plc

For Tracy

Contents

1 Feet   9

2 Posts and Telecommunications   23

3 Poor Darling   38

4 I Was Adored Once Too   56

5 Enough is Too Much Already   79

6 Mrs Tulkinghorne's First Symphony   94

7 Still Life: Remote Control   114

8 A Little Misunderstanding   140

[I]

Unlike the Centre Court at Wimbledon, the Centre Court at our school is the one nobody wants to play on. It is made of asphalt and has dents in it, like Ryvita. All the other courts are grass, out in the sun; Centre Court is in between the science block and the canteen and when there is a Governors' Meeting the governors use it as a car park. The sun only shines on Centre Court at noon in June and there is green algae growing round the edges. When I volunteered to be an umpire at the annual tennis tournament I might have known that I was going to end up on Centre Court.

'You'd better go on Centre Court,' said Mr Evans, 'as it's your first time. It won't matter so much if you make mistakes.' I love Mr Evans. He is so tactful and he looks like an orang-utan in his track suit. I believe myself that he swings from the pipes in the changing room but I haven't personally observed this, you understand.

He just looks as if he might enjoy swinging from things. He has very long arms. Probably he can peel bananas with his toes, which have little tufts of hair on, like beard transplants. I saw them once.

So I was sitting up in my umpire's chair, just like Wimbledon, with an official school pencil and a pad of score cards and I wasn't making any mistakes. This was mainly because they were all first-round matches, the 6–0, 6–0 kind, to get rid of the worst players. All my matches were ladies' doubles which is what you call the fifth- and sixth-year girls when they are playing tennis although not at any other time. We didn't get any spectators except some first-year boys who came to look at the legs and things and Mr Evans, on and off, who was probably there for the same reason.

All the men's matches were on the grass courts, naturally, so I didn't see anything I wanted to see which was Michael Collier. I suppose it was the thought of umpiring Collier that made me put my name down in the first place, before I remembered about ending up on Centre Court. I could only hope that I would be finished in time for the Men's Final so that I could go and watch it because definitely Collier would be in the final. People said that it was hardly worth his while playing, really, why didn't they just give him the trophy and have done with it?

Looking back, I dare say that's what he thought, too.

So anyway, I got rid of all my ladies' doubles and sat around waiting for a mixed doubles. It was cold and windy on Centre Court since it wasn't noon in June, and I wished I had worn a sweater instead of trying to look attractive sort of in short sleeves. Sort of is right. That kind of thing doesn't fool anyone. I had these sandals too which let the draught in something rotten. I should have worn wellies. No one would have noticed. Nobody looks at feet.

After the mixed doubles which was a *fiasco* I thought of going in to get a hot drink – tea or coffee or just boiling water would have done – when I noticed this thing coming down the tramlines and trying to walk on one leg like Richard the Third only all in white.

Richard the Bride.

It was using a tennis racquet head-down as a walking stick which is not done, like cheating at cards. No gentleman would do this to his tennis racquet. This is no gentleman.

'Ho,' says this Richard the Third person. 'Me Carson. You Jane.'

This does not quite qualify as Pun of the Week because he *is* Carson and I *am* Jane. He is Alan Carson from the sixth form – only he is at Oxford now – and he would not know me from Adam only he is a neighbour and used to baby-sit with me once. This is humiliating and I don't tell people.

Carson is known to do a number of strange things and walking on one leg may be one of them for all I know so I do not remark on it.

'Hello, Carson,' I said, very coolly. I was past sounding warm, anyway. 'Where are you going?'

Carson sits down on a stacking chair at the foot of my ladder.

'I'm going to get changed,' he says.

'Did you lose your match?' I say, tactfully like Mr Evans. (I am surprised because he is next most likely after Collier to be in the final.)

'No, I won,' says Carson. 'But it was a Pyrrhic victory,' and he starts whanging the net post with his tennis racquet, boing boing. (This is not good for it either, I should think.)

I have heard about Pyrrhic victories but I do not know what they are.

'What's a Pyrrhic victory?' I said.

'One you can do without,' said Carson. 'Named after King Pyrrhus of Epirus who remarked, after beating the Romans in a battle, "One more win like this and we've had it," on account of the Romans badly chewing up his army.'

'Oh,' I said. 'And did he get another win?'

'Yes,' said Carson. 'But then he got done over at the battle of Beneventum by Curius Dentatus the famous Roman general with funny teeth. Now I just knocked spots off Pete Baldwin in the quarter-final and I'm running up to the net to thank him for a jolly good game old boy, when I turn my ankle and fall flat on my back. It's a good thing,' he added, thoughtfully, 'that I didn't get as far as the net, because I should have jumped over it and *then* fallen flat on my back.'

I could see his point. That's the kind of thing that happens to me.

'I should have met Mick Collier in the semi-final,' said Carson. 'Now he'll have a walk-over. Which should suit him. He doesn't care where he puts his feet.'

'Who will he play in the final?' I say, terribly pleased for Collier as well as being sorry for Carson whose ankle is definitely swelling as even I can see without my glasses which I do not wear in between matches although everyone can see I wear them because of the red mark across my nose.

'Mills or McGarrity,' says Carson. 'Mills is currently beating McGarrity and then Collier will beat Mills – to pulp – and no one will be surprised. I don't know why we bother,' he says, tiredly. 'It was a foregone conclusion,' and he limps away, dragging his injured foot and not even trying to be funny about it because obviously it hurts like hell.

Then it started to rain.

Everybody came and sheltered in the canteen and griped, especially Mills and McGarrity, especially Mills who was within an inch of winning and wanted to get that over and have a crack at Collier who was a more worthy opponent. McGarrity heard all this and looked as if he would like to give Mills a dead leg – or possibly a dead head.

Then it stops raining and Mr Evans the games master and Miss Sylvia Truman who is our lady games master go out and skid about on the grass courts to see if they are safe. They are not. Even then I do not realize what is going to happen because Collier comes over to the dark corner where I am skulking with my cold spotty arms and starts talking to *me*!

'Jane Turner, isn't it?' he says. He must have asked somebody because he couldn't possibly know otherwise. I was only a fourth year then.

And I say, Yes.

And he says, 'I see you every day on the bus, don't I?'

And I say Yes although I travel downstairs and he travels up, among the smokers although of course he doesn't smoke himself because of his athlete's lungs.

And he says, 'You're an umpire today, aren't you?'

And I say Yes.

And he says, 'Do you play?'

And I say Yes which I do and not badly but I don't go in for tournaments because people watch and if I was being watched I would foul it up.

'We have a court at home,' he says which I know because he is a near neighbour like Carson although me and Carson live on the Glebelands Estate and the Colliers live in the Old Rectory. And then he says, '*You ought to come over and play, sometime.*'

And I can't believe this but I say Yes. Yes please. Yes, I'd like that. And I still don't believe it.

And he says, 'Bring your cousin and make up a foursome. That was your cousin who was sitting next to you, wasn't it, on the bus?' and I know he must have been asking about me because my cousin Dawn is only staying with us for a week.

And I say Yes, and he says, 'Come on Friday, then,' and I say Yes. Again. And I wonder how I can last out till Friday evening. It is only three-fifteen on Wednesday.

And then Mr Evans and Miss Sylvia Truman come in from skidding about and Mr Evans, finalist in the All-England Anthropoid Ape Championships says, 'The grass is kaput. We'll have to finish up on Centre Court. Come on Collier. Come on Mills,' and McGarrity says, 'Mills hasn't beaten me yet, Sir,' and Sir says, 'Oh, well,' and doesn't say, 'It's a foregone conclusion,' and Miss Sylvia Truman says, 'Well hurry up and finish him off, Mills,' in a voice that McGarrity isn't supposed to hear but does.

(If Miss Sylvia Truman *was* a man instead of just looking like one, McGarrity would take her apart, but doesn't, because she isn't. Also, she is much bigger than McGarrity.)

And Sir says, 'Where's the umpire?' and I say I am and Sir says, 'Can you manage?' and I say, 'I haven't made any mistakes yet.'

'But it's the *final*,' says Fiery Fred Truman who thinks I am an imbecile – I have heard her – but I say I can manage and I am desperate to do it because of Collier playing and perhaps Sir has been fortifying himself with the flat bottle he thinks we don't know about but which we can see the outline of in his hip pocket, because he says, 'All right, Jane,' and I can't believe it.

But anyway, we all go out to the damp green canyon that is Centre Court and I go up my ladder and Mills finishes off McGarrity love, love, love, love, and still I don't make any mistakes.

And then suddenly *everybody* is there to watch because it is Mills versus Collier and we all want/know that Collier will win.

Collier comes and takes off his sweater and hangs it on the rung of my chair and says, 'Don't be too hard on me, Jane,' with that smile that would make you love him even if you didn't like him, and I say, 'I've got to be impartial,' and he smiles and I wish that I didn't have to be impartial and I am afraid that I won't be impartial.

He says, 'I won't hold it against you, Jane.' And he says, 'Don't forget Friday.'

I say, 'I won't forget Friday,' as loudly as I can so that as many people as possible will hear, which they do.

You can see them being surprised all round the court.

'And don't forget your cousin,' he says, and I say, 'Oh, she's going home on Thursday morning.'

'Some other time, then,' he says.

'No, no,' I said. '*I* can come on Friday,' but he was already walking on to the court and he just looked over his shoulder and said, 'No, it doesn't matter,' and all round the court you could see people not being surprised. And I was up there on that lousy stinking bloody ladder and *everybody* could see me.

I thought I was going to cry and spent a long time putting my glasses on. Collier and Mills began to knock-up and I got out the pencil and the score cards and broke the point off the pencil. I didn't have another one and I didn't want to show my face asking anybody to lend me one so I had to bite the wood away from the lead and of course it didn't have a proper point and made two lines instead of one. And gritty.

And then I remembered that I had to start them off so I said, 'Play, please. Collier to serve.' He had won the toss. Naturally.

My voice had gone woolly and my glasses had steamed over and I was sure people were laughing, even if they weren't. Then I heard this voice down by my feet saying, 'Let him get on with it. If he won't play with you on Friday he can play with himself,' which kind of remark would normally make me go red only I was red already. I looked down and there was Carson looking not at all well because of his foot, probably, but he gave me an evil wink and I remembered that he was a very kind person, really. I remembered that he sometimes gave me a glass of beer when he was baby-sitting. (I was only eleven, then, when he baby-sat. My mother was fussy about leaving us and there was my baby brother as well. He wasn't really sitting with *me*.)

So I smiled and he said, 'Watch the court, for God's sake, they've started,' and they had.

'That's a point to Collier,' he said, and I marked it down and dared not take my eyes off court after that, even to thank him. I looked down again when they changed ends and Carson had gone. (I asked him later where he had gone to and he said he went to throw up. I hope all this doesn't make Carson sound too *coarse*. He was in great pain. It turned out that he had broken a bone in his foot but we didn't know that, then. There are a lot of bones in the foot although you think of it as being solid – down to the toes, at any rate.)

Collier wasn't having it all his own way hooray hooray. Mills was very good too and the first set went to a tie-break. I still wasn't making any mistakes. But when they came off the court after the tie-break which Collier won, and did Wimbledony things with towels and a bit of swigging and spitting, he kept not looking at me. I mean, you could definitely see him *not* looking at me. Everybody could see him *not* looking at me; remembering what he had said about Friday and what I had said about Friday, as loudly as I could.

I was nearly crying again, and what with that and the state of the official school pencil, the score card began to be in a bit of a mess and I suddenly realized that I was putting Collier's points on the wrong line. And of course, I called out, 'Advantage Mills,' when it should have been 40–30 to Collier and he yelled at me to look at what I was doing.

You don't argue with the umpire. You certainly don't *yell* at the umpire, but he did. I know I was wrong but he didn't have to yell. I kept thinking about him yelling and about Friday and in the next game I made the same mistake again and he was saying, 'That's all I need; a cross-eyed umpire. There's eight hundred people in this school can't we find *one* with twenty–twenty vision?' If Fiery Fred or Orang-Evans had heard he might not have, but he was up by the net and facing away from them. He got worse and worse. Abusive.

Then Mills won the next game without any help from me and I thought, At least he's not having another walk-over, and I remembered what Carson had said. 'He doesn't care where he puts his feet.' And of course, after that, I couldn't help looking at his feet and Carson was right. He didn't care where he put them. He had this very fantastic service that went up about ten yards before he hit the ball, but his toes were over the base line three times out of five. I don't know why nobody noticed. I suppose they were all watching the fantastic ten-yard service and anyway, nobody looks at feet.

At first I forgot that this was anything to do with me; when I did remember I couldn't bear to do anything about it, at first. Then it was Mills who was serving and I had time to think.

I thought, Why should he get away with it?

Then I thought, He gets away with everything, and I realized that Carson probably hadn't been talking about real feet but feet was all I could think of.

Collier served. His feet were not where they should have been.

'Fifteen–love.'

I thought, I'll give you one more chance, because he was playing so well and I didn't want to spoil that fantastic service. But he had his chance, and he did it again. It was a beautiful shot, an ace, right down the centre line, and Mills never got near it.

I said, 'Foot fault.'

There was a sort of mumbling noise from everyone watching and Collier scowled but he had to play the second service. Mills tipped it back over the net and Collier never got near it.

'Fifteen all.'

'Foot fault.'

He was going to argue but of course he couldn't because feet is not what he looked at when he was serving.

'Fifteen–thirty.' His second service wasn't very good, really.

'Foot fault.'

'Fifteen–forty.'

And then he did begin to look, and watching his feet he had to stop watching the ball and all sorts of things began to happen to his service.

Mills won that set.

'What the hell are you playing at, Turner?' said Collier, when they came off court and he called me a vindictive little cow while he was towelling and spitting but honestly, I never called foot fault if it wasn't one.

They went back for the third set and it was Collier's service. He glared at me like he had death-ray eyeballs and tossed up the first ball. And looked up.

And looked down at his feet.

And looked up again, but it was too late and the ball came straight down and bounced and rolled away into the crowd.

So he served again, looked up, looked down, and tried to move back and trod on his own foot and fell over.

People laughed. A laugh sounds terrible on Centre Court with all those walls to bounce off. Some of the algae had transferred itself to his shorts.

By now, *everybody* was looking at his feet.

He served a double fault.

'So who's winning?' said Alan Carson, back again and now looking greener than Collier's shorts. I knew he would understand because he *had* come back instead of going home to pass out which was what he should have been doing.

'I am,' I said, miserably.

'Two Pyrrhic victories in one afternoon?' said Alan. 'That must be some kind of a record.'

'It must be,' I said. 'It's got a hole in it.'

[2]

Posts and Telecommunications

There was no point in writing letters; he was too busy to answer them, except by occasional postcards that arrived without stamps, mailed through the office Addressograph.

'Surely it's nicer to talk to each other properly?' he said, and made sure that she had extra pocket money to pay for the calls.

'It's not talking properly,' she protested. 'It's just noises that sound like us. I've got this book that shows you how it works.'

She explained the diagrams, very efficiently, she thought, but it made no difference. Still he did not write.

Isobel's dislike of telephones was indiscriminate, but her deepest animosity was directed at the vandal-proof pay phone in the school's dark lobby, stuck to the wall under a perspex hood that curved over her head like a monstrous hair-drier. Since the dictionary yielded no term for an irrational fear and hatred of telephones, she referred to her condition as telephobia, liking the sound of it and not understanding its literal meaning which was more accurate than she knew. The fear went back a long way, to the days in the Balham flat, when the telephone had stood in the corner of the hall on a little three-legged table that, although low, was nevertheless high enough to set the instrument exactly on a level with Isobel's chin. Her only memories of the flat were of the red-stained glass panels in the front door and, as she approached the door, of the telephone springing out with shrill cries, like a killer chihuahua, trained to go for the ear. But in those days there had at least been a human hand to still the beast. It was after the withdrawing of the hand that the hatred set in.

During the first weeks at school she had rung her father every evening, weeping into the receiver and begging to be fetched home again. By now the telephone was ringing in Richmond instead of Balham. He did not answer the summons instantly, as her mother would have done, and as the couplets drilled into her ear she could visualize him, hurrying in from the garden – for it was a fine autumn and he would be passing his little leisure in pottering – discarding his gloves, wiping his feet and clearing his throat preliminary to lifting the hand set.

'Hullo? John Elder speaking. Who is –?'

'Daddy!'

'Oh, Isobel.' By the end of her second week at school he was beginning to sigh when he heard her choking, a hundred miles away.

'Daddy, I want to come home.'

'Listen, darling . . .'

'I want to *see* you . . .'

'I'll be coming up in a fortnight, you know I will.'

'I want to see you *now*. I want to come home!'

'Isobel, Isobel,' he said, professionally patient. He was a businessman, but he brought professionalism to all his doings, a professional father, almost. 'Darling, aren't they kind to you?'

'Yes.' They were as kind as three hundred people could be collectively kind. 'But I want you.'

He tried firmness. 'You must be making it very hard for them, Is.'

'I don't care. I hate it here . . .'

He tried bluntness. His timing was impeccable. 'Isobel, you're too old for this. If you were a boy you could have been packed off at seven.'

'You wouldn't have –'

'No, of course I wouldn't, but some people –'

'It's cruel to do that. It's cruel!'

'Isobel!' Wilfully misunderstanding, he rebuked her, and she was wrong-footed.

'I didn't mean you, but –'

'I know you didn't.' His voice softened again, in the knowledge that he was winning. She was arguing now instead of crying, so reason must prevail.

They were both very reasonable when he arrived, a fortnight later. They drove out for lunch.

'Look, my love,' he said, over the lemon sorbets, 'if you don't stay here it'd mean living with Granny.'

'Couldn't she live with us?'

'She wouldn't want to. Too independent.' He lied in his teeth. 'It'd be Sandringham Gardens or nothing. Do you really want that?'

'Doesn't Granny want *me*?'

'Of *course* she does,' he said, heartily. Granny then was out of the question. Isobel had not seen her since the funeral when she had stood at the graveside peering askance at the other mourners as if seeking her daughter's murderer among them, although Mummy had died quite naturally, although slowly.

'I wouldn't be a nuisance at home. I could be a – a –' she searched for the alien phrase picked up from a newspaper, '– a latchkey kid.'

'No, sweetheart, it wouldn't do. I can't have you hanging around the house alone.'

'I'd be at school all day, and you'd be home in the evenings.'

'Not always,' he said. 'And what about the holidays?'

'What about an au pair?' she asked, making a last effort.

'I can't have an au pair hanging around the place with *me*.' He laughed. Too simple and too sad to see the joke, she laughed with him.

After this her phone calls dwindled to Wednesdays and weekends. One evening when she rang a woman answered, giving no name but uncertainly quoting the number. Isobel was too surprised to speak.

'Who's there?' the woman asked.

'Who are you?' Isobel cried. 'Where's Daddy?'

'You must be Isobel.' The voice was decently nervous and conciliatory. 'I can see your photograph from here.'

Isobel ground her teeth. The photograph stood on the mantelpiece in the living room. Daddy must have had an extension installed. 'I'd like to speak to my father, please.'

'He's just coming.'

He'd better be.

'Who's that woman?' Isobel demanded, when she heard the receiver change hands.

'Marion Hollis. She's a friend. I'm taking her out to dinner.'

You're going to marry her, thought Isobel, aged eleven. Isobel aged fourteen now knew this to have been a typically childish and naïve assumption, but it had turned out after a year to be right. They had the good sense to wed in the holidays, when she could be present, instead of doing it furtively, on the quiet, as her friend Stephanie had predicted. Granny stood beside her in the register office, waxing fat on the certainty that her homicidal suspicions had been proven. She was one station in life removed from folding her arms, clicking her teeth and munching her grief (Avis is hardly cold in her grave!) but she marred the reception by fawning on Isobel and putting a trembling arm round her shoulders every time Marion looked in their direction. Isobel betrayed her by basely falling in love with Marion.

'Marion's lovely,' she said to her friend Stephanie, so often that in the end Stephanie turned brutal and retorted, 'You only think that because you hardly ever see her. It'd be different if you were living at home. Wait till the Christmas holidays,' Stephanie said.

Christmas was good.

'It's almost like having Mummy back, with Marion there,' Isobel said. It was not, but this was the only comparable pleasure that she could think of.

'Do you call her Mummy?' Stephanie's narrow face became positively two-dimensional.

'Of course not. I call her Marion. Mummy promised me I could have my ears pierced when I was twelve, and I told Marion and she took me to have it done herself, and bought me these.'

Isobel hooked back her hair to display gold studs.

'All studs are gold plate, except the really cheapo ones.'

'These are gold right through,' Isobel said. 'Eighteen carat. Marion said it was important to have real gold when your ears are first pierced because –'

'Wait till she has a baby,' Stephanie said.

Marion was in no hurry to have a baby. Isobel asked her outright one evening, over the telephone, and Marion laughed happily, in Richmond.

'I'm not thirty, yet. There's plenty of time. I want to go on working for a bit.'

Stephanie explained that if you waited too long to have your first child it could be deformed.

Marion worked for a publisher. She sent Isobel fat Jiffy-bags full of books, sometimes weeks before they were published. When Isobel rang to thank her Marion was quick to lift the receiver as though she knew who was calling. It did not seem to matter how often she telephoned, Marion was always there to answer, always pleased to talk.

'She's just relieved that you're accepting her.'

Isobel, who had been reading a suggestive book on the occult that Marion had packed by mistake, made a wax image of Stephanie out of a specially purchased black candle. It had a forked tongue, and when Isobel melted it down the tongue went first, but Stephanie and her own bifurcated organ flourished unimpaired.

After a happy chat with Marion, Isobel would ask for her father. Sometimes he came to the telephone at once, as if he had only been waiting for Marion to relinquish the receiver, but occasionally he was not there at all.

'He's travelling a lot, these days,' Marion explained.

'Don't you miss him?'

'Of course I do, but he'll be back on Friday.'

He was definitely supposed to be back for half term, but in the end Isobel and Marion spent it on their own, tramping round all the London museums by day and visiting theatres in the evening.

'I'm not sure you should be seeing this,' Marion fretted, more than once, during some seamy drama insufficiently researched beforehand. Privately Isobel agreed, and armed herself with ammunition to sling at Stephanie who, for all her worldly wisdom, had seen little more than Shakespeare and pantomimes.

Over the following eighteen months, her father's absences lengthened.

'He'll be back next Friday,' Marion would say, and then, 'He'll be back the week after next.' Finally, 'I'm not sure exactly when he'll be back.'

'That doesn't sound too good,' Stephanie remarked, smiling. 'Perhaps they're breaking up.'

'Marion's not worried,' Isobel said. She had lately discovered, by oblique investigation, some facts about Stephanie's own home circumstances and, prompted by Marion, was inclined to be generous. Stephanie's barbs became blunt, and her stings easily withdrawn. In any case, Marion's unconcern was genuine. She had recently been promoted to editor, and her work was demanding.

'I wouldn't ring before eight,' she cautioned, one evening. 'I get off so late, these days. What would you like for your birthday?'

'From you or from Dad?'

'Either or both. Fourteen's special.'

'Is it?'

'It was when I was fourteen. The last big one before twenty-one.'

'Eighteen's the big one now. You can vote.'

'Fourteen's still special.' Marion could make anything sound special. 'Choose whatever you like.'

A desire to test them overcame Isobel. 'I could do with a micro.'

'Micro what?'

'Computer. We've got plenty of machines here, but everyone wants to use them and they've got awfully small memories, really. I need a 32 K for what I'm doing.' She named a machine that was far beyond the capacity of anything the school could offer, in spite of the fees, and on her birthday it arrived. She unpacked the box on her bed, under the censorious eyes of Stephanie and other friends. The friends could find nothing to fault, especially when a second, much larger box turned out to contain a portable television set.

The telly's for visual display – they said you would need it. How about a printer for Christmas? All our love, Dad and Marion, said the note slipped into her birthday card. The note and the signatures were in Marion's hand, as was the card.

'Step-mum's coughing up,' said a friend, enviously.

'Buying you off,' Stephanie mouthed, not realizing how Marion would have trekked from shop to shop in her small spare time, questing and questioning because she did not read the magazines that would have told her all she needed to know.

Isobel did not wait until after eight to ring home this evening, and took a chance that Marion would have got off early. The phone buzzed twice, then a formal, strangely embarrassed impersonation of her father's voice articulated, 'John and Marion Elder are out at the moment. If you would like to leave a message after the pips sound, we'll get back to you as soon as we can.'

Isobel had no message. The pips squeaked, but her joyful unframed thanks degenerated from incoherence to total silence. For a moment she stood under the perspex canopy, listening to the silence in Richmond, then put down the receiver. Her hand was shaking. It was only the sight of Stephanie, prowling down the corridor, that reactivated her. She paid in the coins, dialled and waited. Stephanie drew level. A voice in her ear said, unemphatically, 'John and Marion Elder are out at the moment. If you would like to leave a message after the pips sound, we'll get back to you as soon as we can.'

Isobel could see Stephanie still, reflected in the perspex, lurking. When the voice stopped and the pips sounded, she clasped the hand set fervently and cried, 'Oh Daddy, darling Marion, thank you *so* much! I never *guessed* you'd get it, and the television, it's lovely, everyone's *green* . . .' Stephanie was still there. She paused, as if to let the listening party answer, and plunged on, 'They just couldn't *believe* it when I unpacked, it's *wonderful*, no one else has got such *marvellous* parents, I don't know what to say . . .'

This was becoming more distressingly evident with every mouthful. She had never heard such drivel, never imagined that she could produce such a noise. Stephanie had gone. Isobel hung up, shaking all over, now. She could picture the answering machine on the glass-topped table beside the telephone, with her dreadful gush locked into its unforgiving spools. Marion, when she came home at eight, would play it back and think she had gone right off her head, if indeed she could make out who was speaking, but it was after nine before Marion responded. Isobel was heading for the bathroom when a prefect came complaining up the back stairs to fetch her.

'You know you're not supposed to get calls this late, but as it's your birthday . . .' News of the amazing present had spread round the school.

Isobel ran past her, down the stairs.

'It's your step-mother.'

Marion was contrite. 'Isobel, love, I'm sorry I was out when you rang. Happy birthday.'

'I didn't know you'd got an answering machine.'

'It only came yesterday. I'm sorry, I should have warned you. Did everything arrive safely?'

'Oh yes – I only wanted to thank you.'

'I'm so sorry. I got stuck at this ghastly party. Forty authors and all of them drunk –'

'Is Dad there?'

'Oh, Isobel, I'm sorry. He's flying out to Athens in the morning, so he'll go straight to Heathrow from the office and stay overnight. He'll be so sorry –'

Methinks the lady doth protest too much, Isobel murmured, making her way upstairs again.

After a week or two she could no longer remember exactly when she had last spoken to her father. He was in Bonn, Copenhagen, New York, and Marion, evidently depressed at the prospect of returning to an empty house, stayed out later and later. More often than not, when Isobel dialled the Richmond number, there was no one to lift the receiver and her only reply was the echo of her father enunciating shiftily, 'John and Marion Elder are out at the moment. If you would like to leave a message after the pips sound, we'll get back to you as soon as we can.' The longed-for end of term looked uncomfortably close. She thought of Stephanie who, too often, on the happy brink of a holiday, had been suddenly dispatched to her cousins in Taunton. Were John and Marion Elder planning that she should spend her Easter with Gran, still winnowing her sorrows with gleeful anguish? When the machine spoke she refused to answer; when she lifted the receiver now she scarcely expected human contact, so one evening she was struck speechless when her father's living voice, and not its phantom, addressed her.

'Isobel! You must be psychic! I was just going to ring you . . . my hand was on the phone.'

'Oh.' She could say nothing else.

'Are you there?'

'Yes, Dad.'

'Look, darling, something's come up. I've got to go to Athens again next week, and Marion's getting ready for Bologna.'

'Where?'

'Bologna. The Book Fair. You must have heard her mention it. Anyway, she's stopping off in Paris on the way back, to see her sister. Look, would you mind awfully if you spent the first couple of weeks of the holiday with Gran?'

She wailed, like the child of three years ago, 'But I want to come home! I've been looking forward –'

'But there'll be no one here.'

'I can manage, I'm fourteen now, remember. I don't need anyone with me.'

'But there won't be anyone here at all, for a fortnight. Look, love, Marion'll be back on the second Friday. She'll drive over and collect you. You'll have the last week together.'

'She needn't bother. I don't want to see either of you!' Isobel slammed the hand set back into its cradle. She waited all evening for her chastened parent to call and beg forgiveness, but she had failed to move him. All that came was a carefully reasoned letter, two days later, reminding her that she was old enough now to accept hard knocks, and enclosing the rail fare to Gran's, with double that amount in pocket money to purchase her silence.

Buying you off, said a spiteful voice that was not Stephanie's.

At Gran's she caught a cold. The house in Sandringham Gardens was conducive to ill health, where the miasma of Gran's cultivated woe hung low like an unwholesome mist over a fen. Gran, unable to cope with more than one misfortune at a time, and so deeply absorbed in her own obscure grievance that she could scarcely comprehend another, much less assuage it, administered viscous cough syrup from the back of the bathroom cabinet, and went out to inflict herself on a neighbour. Isobel lay in bed and cried desultorily through the vacant morning. When noon came and Gran had not returned, she wrapped a shawl round her nightdress and limped down to the telephone, a post-war Bakelite model with a moist bloom on the mouth piece. Her whole body ached in sympathy with her throat, and she arranged herself very comfortably in an armchair before lifting the receiver. The familiar tones announced that John and Marion Elder were elsewhere. Isobel waited for the pips, swallowed painfully, and began.

'John, darling John, I've got to see you. Why don't you call me any more? It's three weeks . . . something awful's happened . . . I can't tell Mummy. I feel so miserable – and sick – I wish I could see you, please John, darling. Let's meet again. I must talk to you properly, I can't bear these machines. Oh darling, what am I going to do?'

She had meant to stop there, but amazed and appalled by the ease with which it came out she spoke again.

'I've got to talk to someone . . . before I see the doctor. Don't leave me now. I didn't mean it about you being old, I *didn't*, but I'm only fourteen. I never told you that, did I? Mummy will kill me. I don't know what Daddy will say. Oh John, darling, call me as soon as you get home from Cannes – it was Cannes you were going to, wasn't it? You know the number . . . call after eight . . .'

The effort of talking had exhausted her and she coughed for a long time after hanging up. Her voice was so hoarse and tearful that she hardly recognized it as her own. Nor would Marion recognize it, when she came home from Paris that evening and played back the tape.

[3]

Poor Darling

'I can quite well manage the suitcase,' she cried, seeing him bent sideways by the weight.

'No,' he said. 'I'll carry it.' He did not want to watch her struggling. He liked to see her stride, coat swinging, perfect balance maintained. Who would have thought such little feet could walk all by themselves and carry a full-grown woman? Her heels bit down hard on the hard surface of the platform and Adam expected to see a row of tiny hoofprints appear, with exquisite precision, one in front of the other.

Connie slapped along beside her, a wonderful object of comparison. Anyone would look exquisite, set next to Connie.

'This will do, won't it, Con? Open the door, darling. Darling, the door.' Adam turned the handle and the little hooves went up, hopskip, while Connie pancaked behind and he was left to close the door and shunt the suitcase into the compartment.

'Not in the rack, darling. You'll ruin yourself. There's a little *place* between the seats.'

Adam pursued the case along the gangway, steering it with his toe, but the compartment was already full and there was another suitcase in the little place, squatting there like a toad in a hole.

'It'll have to go up above,' said Connie, cigarette already plugged in and exhaling toxic fumes. She yanked the suitcase off the floor and rammed it into the overhead rack. Simultaneously the train jerked into motion and for a disagreeable moment Connie seemed to be swinging from the roof.

'Whoohoops!' cried Connie, an unidentified primate, ululating through the jungle from tree to tree.

'Sit *down*, Connie. Sit down, darling. Sit by me.' She gathered up the fur-collared coat which, without her inside it, had collapsed from exhaustion.

'Have the window seat,' said Connie, walloping him into place, much as she had dealt with the suitcase. He sat by the window and Connie settled into folds beside him. Across the table his mother reactivated herself. The feet were at rest; the hands came into play. They opened her handbag to fetch out cigarettes, lighter and purse.

'I suppose one can get a drink on these things?'

'Just sit still for a moment,' said Connie. 'I'll go along to the buffet and get you a coffee.'

'I don't know that I want one, just yet. You go and get yourself a coffee, Con. No, Adam will get one for you, won't you darling?'

'I'll go in a minute,' said Connie. 'I can wait. You sit there and get your breath back.'

'Adam can go and see if there's somewhere to get a drink. It might be miles down the train. You don't mind, do you, darling? No, wait a moment. It might be in the other direction. We were in such a hurry I didn't notice.'

A young man leaned across the gangway.

'It's in the next carriage but one – that way – through First Class.'

She did not look at him. His assistance had not been invited. 'I wonder if there's anywhere to sit. There may be a dining car.'

'There's a buffet car,' said the young man. 'They don't serve meals on this train.'

'You'd better go and look, darling.' She continued to

stare widely away from the young man and he went back to reading his magazine.

'No rush,' said Connie. 'Let's wait until we both want one.'

'Just go and look, darling.'

'Sit down, Adam,' said Connie. 'I'll go in a moment.'

'Have you got a cigarette, Con? Oh no, not one of those disgusting things. Where on earth are mine? I must have dropped them in the taxi. Do you think they sell them in the buffet?'

'Yours are on the table,' said Connie.

'So they are – oh, it's an empty packet. Darling, run along and see if they have any. You can get Connie's coffee at the same time.'

'I'll go,' said Connie, massively immovable. 'Have one of mine. They aren't so bad if you keep your eyes shut.'

'They smell like a fire in a potato clamp. No no; oh, darling, do get a move on,' she said.

'Can I have some money?' said Adam.

'Money?' Adam felt that he had dropped a stone into a limpid pool and fouled it. 'What happened to that pound I gave you?'

'I had to pay for the taxi. Connie only had a fiver.'

'But a pound? It can't be a pound from Cannon Street.'

'I had to give him a tip.'

'I suppose I must owe you a pound then, darling.'

'I've still only got a fiver,' said Connie.

'I haven't got any money at all,' said Adam. Hands opened purse.

'Well, here's another pound. Now, do hurry up, darling.'
Adam took the note and climbed over the rolling dunes
and lush valleys of Connie's lap.

'Just the one coffee, darling, and twenty King Size. Any
kind.'

'Can I have a Coke?'

'Oh, darling. Tooth rot.'

'Can I?'

'Damn, the flint's gone. Have you got any flints, Con?'

Adam swayed along the corridor, past the First Class
compartments, chivied by a silent chant:

> *Damn, the flint's gone.*
> *Have you got any flints, Con?*

Con. Connie Hipps. Lucy and Jonathan called her the
Hippo, Rose Hipps; Simon, with his taste for the arcane,
preferred the Hippogryph. Adam, however, could see that
it was foolish to try and improve on perfection, like carving
cameos on a meringue, for Connie began with a very small
head, went down and relentlessly out, and then in again,
abruptly dwindling away towards the ankles. She would
spin very nicely on either end.

He found the buffet car laid out like a café, with formica-
topped tables. The Coke came in a tin, but Connie's coffee
expanded to a paper carton, lumps of wrapped sugar, a
spoon, a smaller carton of milk. He stowed it all about his
person and went back to his carriage. 'Look! No hands!'

'Oh, darling, wasn't there a buffet after all?' On his

behalf, accusing, she looked at last towards the young man, but he was asleep. Silently, Adam began to unpack himself. The coffee carton was in his right pocket, the can of Coke in his left. The milk was up his sleeve and the sugar in the hip pocket of his jeans. The spoon nestled under his watch strap and he had tucked the straw for the Coke behind his ear. His mother began to laugh.

'Oh, darling, you are priceless. Look at him, Con. Darling, where are my cigarettes?'

'A pound wasn't enough. Everything's gone up.'

'I see you bought your Coke, though. Where's the change?'

'Here. Can I keep it towards *my* pound?'

'No. I'll give that to you when we arrive. Will another twenty be enough?'

'Yes.'

'I think you should pay for the Coke yourself. It's ruinous.'

'I haven't got any *money*.' He went for the cigarettes, colliding in the doorway with a woman, one of the itinerant passengers who were still ranging up and down the train looking for a seat. When he returned he found that she was sitting next to his mother. She had clearly made an unsolicited effort to be pleasant, since his mother was staring out of the window. The fur-collared coat was piled on the table as a sign of silent reproach to the woman who had taken its place.

Connie ripped the lid from her coffee carton and began

to add things to it. The plastic spoon melted and curled up.

'British rubbish,' said Connie, trying to bite the spoon back into shape.

'Peter said we ought to travel First Class. I didn't think it would be worth it on such a short journey. I didn't realize we'd be so cramped. My change, darling; don't be sly. You'll get your money at Norwich. Darling, what are you doing with those cards? I must have been mad to come up without Peter. He can't get away until tomorrow.'

'You said we could have a game,' said Adam.

'What about the others?'

'Lucy and the boys aren't coming till Friday.'

'Well, can we?'

'What, darling?'

'Play cards. You said we could play cards. You said you'd like to.'

'All right, darling. It'll be a hell of a squeeze but I suppose we shall make out. We're really only keeping the house on for holidays. After the wedding we shall be in Town, most of the time.'

'Will you keep the flat?'

'Oh, darling, wait a moment. No, didn't I tell you? I've already had an offer for it.'

'You'll miss having somewhere of your own after all this time,' said Connie. She knocked the end off her cigarette and began foraging among her skirts after it.

'Sally's given me first refusal of her cottage. It's on Rollesby Broad. She wants thirty thousand for it, though.'

'That shack?'

'It's worth it – to me. I've been alone for seven years. I must have somewhere to preserve something of myself.'

Alone? Adam thought. Where was I, then?

'I'm sure I'm on fire.'

'Poker?'

'What?'

'Shall we play poker? Look, I've got all these half-pennies.'

'I won't play for money, darling.'

'It's not real money.'

'He's right,' said Connie. 'It's not real money. Can you smell burning?'

'I've been saving them,' said Adam. 'Every time I get some change I put the halfpence aside.'

'I thought you said you hadn't got any money.'

'It's not real money. What about pontoon?'

'I won't play for money. The garden goes right down to the water's edge. It's a ninety-foot frontage. Half an acre.'

'Simon doesn't mind playing for money,' said Adam.

'Darling, I'm not Simon. We'll play snap.' He guessed that she wanted a game where she could go on talking. She was so nervous. He was anguished by her nervousness.

'Shall I deal?'

'Please, darling. You know, Con, Simon's marvellous with him – a real story-book big brother. I was so afraid that none of them would get on, but it's working out wonderfully. Jonathan's practically Adam's best friend. Of course, they hardly ever meet.'

'Suppose they hadn't got on?'

'Oh, Adam gets on with everyone. He's so conciliatory.'

Adam began to deal three hands.

'Not me,' said Connie. He started again. Simon and Jonathan were about to become his step-brothers, Lucy his step-sister. His mother often said that he was called Adam because his father had insisted, although Adam's memory of his father did not include insistence. He imagined that she was glad now, because it had turned out to be the right sort of name. He was also called Ivor, his father's own name, and that wasn't all right at all. It was being quietly disposed of, along with the flat, the louche friends, seven years hard without a man. Bye-bye Mrs Owen, the Welshman's widow.

She never called him Adam to his face, or Ivor, always Darling. For seven years he had taken it for granted, as his due. Now he was one of four darlings and felt diminished. The endearment had become a coin of no value, like the despised halfpennies, not real money.

'I dealt. You start,' he said.

They played one game and Adam lost; another, and Adam lost again.

'You're lucky today,' he said. 'It must have been that ladder you didn't walk under at Liverpool Street.'

'He's an awfully good loser,' she said. 'Jonathan beats

him at everything and he never minds.' (Be nice to Jonathan, darling. He still misses his mother terribly. Oh terribly. Terrible. He could understand that.)

'Why's it called Liverpool Street? It's nowhere near Liverpool.' It was not worth beating Jonathan at anything. He raised hell if you did.

'Well, darling, Oxford Street's nowhere near Oxford, is it? I expect it was named after Lord Liverpool.'

'Was there a Lord Liverpool?' It sounded phony, like Lord Broadstairs, Lord Charing Cross.

'It would hardly be named after Bert Liverpool, would it?' said Connie, under the impression that Bert was a name favoured by the Common Man.

'Oh darling, I don't think I can play another game just yet. Would you like to run along to the buffet? I think I'd quite enjoy that coffee, now.'

She was speaking more and more loudly. Adam knew why. The train was aimed at the rural bulge of East Anglia and the three men in the seats behind, owners of the toad suitcase, were chatting in amiable but alien accents.

Best you do . . . that don't . . . I aren't arguing . . .

Her voice became sharper and more Southern with every sentence, as though she feared that the deep green country would swallow her up into an unmarked grave, unless she kept her flag flying.

'Darling, you don't mind going again, do you? Connie, do you want another cup – well, it's not exactly a *cup*, is it?'

Connie shook her head and grunted. Adam climbed over her, to the gangway.

'What about the money?' he said, and struck a gangster pose. 'Where's da mazuma?'

'Darling!' She was affronted. 'You don't mind going, do you?'

'Of course not. But I haven't got any money.'

'What about all those halfpence?'

'I can't give them that. They'd think I was trying to be funny.'

'Yes, darling. You do try, don't you?'

'Anyway, it's my poker money.' She opened her purse and counted out coins. He began to leave.

'He's awfully sullen sometimes, Con. I sometimes wonder . . .'

He bobbed back again.

'Sugar?'

'Darling, you know I never do. Now, push off.' *Push off* came out through a smile full of teeth. He had struck a false note; a whole cacophony of false notes, and he had been so careful. He walked all a-jangle down the First Class corridor. Perhaps it was Connie, and not him. He had nothing against Connie, but he wished that she had travelled separately. She was not wanted on voyage, and it was the last voyage, the very last.

Connie was asleep by the time he came back, head bouncing like a football in a string bag, and gargling sonorously. He struggled into his seat and pushed the coffee across the table. His mother appeared to notice him with a start.

'Darling, where have you been?'

'I had to queue.' He did not mention that he had walked to the other end of the train first, to see if anyone would remark his absence. It had been remarked.

'Do you want another game yet?'

'Don't nag, darling.' She lit a cigarette and reclined in the little space available, glancing, between drags, at the interloping woman who had occupied the adjacent seat. Adam dealt himself a hand of patience and watched her also. He had thought at first that she was middle-aged. Her hair was greying and a groove ran vertically between her eyebrows as if her forehead had been made in two halves and pushed together; but her clothes were not grandmotherly. They were the kind of clothes his mother wore at weekends when there was no one to see – or had done, before there was anyone to look. She would never have worn them on a train, these haphazard layers of cotton and corduroy. The woman was reading a book and making notes in a folder on her lap, since there was no room on the table for a folder and the fur-collared coat.

Adam plucked idly at the patience. His mother lit another cigarette and Connie honked fitfully like a distant locomotive, belting across the prairie wastes. The woman turned her book face-down and took off her glasses, rubbing her eyes. Adam saw then that she could be no older than his mother, only more weathered. It seemed to him very sad that anyone so young should be so well worn, and he began to look, as he always did at plain and ageing women, to see if she had a wedding ring, as it seemed even sadder that such people should be alone as well. Of course, they might be widowed, but at least they had had someone once . . .

He saw the ring, and something else. She was missing the two top joints from the two middle fingers of her left hand. He glanced away quickly, but not quickly enough. His mother followed his eyes, as *she* always did when they were about their own business, and saw the lopped hand resting on the book. The woman looked nowhere in particular. Possibly she was accustomed to people staring at her hand and no longer cared. Without her glasses she saw nothing, he hoped.

'Darling?'

'Yes?'

'Would you like another game of cards? Connie's dead to the world.'

'All right,' he said, unsuspecting. 'The patience won't come out.'

'I'll deal, shall I?'

He was not unsuspecting for long. His mother's intelligent fingers deliberately crushed the coffee carton and flicked it aside. Then they rounded up the scattered cards, sifting, riffling, trilling. Look how clever we are. We can do everything that's expected of us, and we're *all here*!

'You lay first, darling.'

He slapped a Queen of Hearts on to the table and she covered it with a Queen of Spades, fingers pouncing and then flicking up, skittishly.

'Snap, darling. Wake up.'

Seven of Diamonds, Two of Clubs, Queen of Clubs, Six of Diamonds, Nine of Hearts, Nine of Spades. She was a lousy shuffler, for all the fingers.

'Snap, darling. Are you falling asleep like poor Connie?'

No one could fall asleep like poor Connie. She wallowed in slumber, open-mouthed.

Two of Spades.

King of Diamonds.

Three of Clubs.

King of Spades.

King of Clubs.

'Snap, darling.'

He wanted the game over and missed every call. The fingers skipped up and down, especially, he thought, the ring fingers. On the left hand the new engagement ring. On the right, being discreetly phased out, the old engagement ring, the old wedding ring. On Saturday, he supposed, they would disappear altogether.

Eight of Diamonds.

Eight of Hearts.

'Snap!'

Ace of Diamonds. Ace of Clubs.

'Snap!'

The woman gazed nowhere. Surely she could see what

was going on? He wanted to explain. Excuse me, my mother's not doing it on purpose. She doesn't mean to. Nervous . . .

'Snap. Darling, you're getting terribly sulky. It's no good expecting to win if you don't attend.'

An admonitory finger waved under his nose. But I assure you, madam, there's no harm in it. Just –

'You said I was an awfully good loser. I don't mind losing.'

'It's no good being an awfully good loser if you don't even try to win.'

'Better than trying to win and being a bad loser,' he said, thinking of Jonathan.

'I don't think I want to play with you any more,' she said, tossing down the cards. 'You're getting very waspish.' The hands had had their outing and lay recovering on the table.

Adam looked at the other hands alongside, but the woman was still staring at nothing. Then the magazine slid off the lap of the sleeping young man and fell to the floor. There was an LP filed inside it and they landed with a thump. The young man, not asleep after all, sat up startled and groped for them, but the woman bent down to pick them up, and returned them to him; so calmly proffering them in her mutilated hand.

'I see you have the best recording,' she said.

He looked pleased. 'Do you think so?'

'Oh yes. Sometimes any good performance will do,

especially if you're hard up; but it has to be Ashkenazy for this one, hard up or not.'

'Oh *yes*,' he said, cradling his record, properly awake now and eager. They began to talk, quietly, across the gangway. Adam could hear nothing but he saw everything. Even a tired untidy woman with a smashed hand could make a young man smile. His mother watched them too. She had missed her chance to make a young man smile. She leaned across the table and poked Connie, unkindly.

'Wake up, Con. You know you always feel terrible if you sleep too long on trains.'

Connie opened her eyes, snorting and blinking.

'Uaaah?'

'I said, you always feel terrible if you sleep on trains.'

'Do I?' Connie sounded bewildered. 'I wasn't properly asleep. What was that last stop? Ipswich?'

'Manningtree. We're coming into Ipswich now.'

'I knew we'd stopped somewhere,' said Connie, on the defensive. 'Just dozing.' She burrowed for cigarettes. 'Oh God, now I've run out, too.'

'Have one of mine. Adam, would you mind going along to the buffet *again* to get Mrs Hipps some *more* cigarettes?'

'I'll go,' said Connie. They were both out of favour now and sat side by side, under small personal clouds, looking out of the window.

'Well, aren't you going?'

He stood up.

'It's all right. I'll go,' said Connie, as he squeezed past.

'I don't mind. Really.'

'You minded when I asked you to fetch my coffee,' said his mother. 'Don't imagine that you're going to be waited on hand and foot just because I've given up working. You'd better give him some money, Con, before he demands it with menaces.'

Ladies and gentlemen. This is really a joke. She's my mother. We understand each other . . .

'Here's the fiver,' said Connie.

'Don't lose the change,' said his mother. 'Don't stand there in the aisle.'

The train had stopped again and people were trying to push past him on the way out, among them the woman and the young man.

'Get out of the way, Adam, for heaven's sake. You may *be* an idiot but you don't have to prove it.'

He dodged into the First Class corridor, wondering how the other three darlings would take to becoming errand boys. He did it for love. She did not love *them* and did not pretend to. They got along. That was enough. That was civilized.

When he reached the buffet car he found two people ahead of him at the bar; the woman and the young man, buying beer. He felt that he should approach them and explain. Not to apologize, but merely to clarify the situation. You see, she didn't mean to be unkind about your hand. It's not unkindness. But she compares herself with people and she has to be best. She has to be perfect. You can see that, can't you? Perfect. She's my mother. I understand her. Excuse me, it's hard to explain, excuse me . . .

They were buying sandwiches too.

'Do you want to take this lot back to the compartment?' said the young man.

'I'd as soon stay here. There's plenty of room and I don't think I can sit and listen to that bitch of a woman all the way to Norwich.'

'I did hope Darling might do her in,' said the young man, 'but I went to sleep and when I woke up – Jesus! She was still at it. I don't like to see children crucified in public.'

'Perhaps he'll push her out on a quiet stretch,' said the woman. Carrying their beer and sandwiches they moved to a vacant table, never knowing that he stood there. 'What a pity we're not going North. There's that lovely viaduct at Durham – she'd never survive the drop.'

'What had the poor little devil done, anyway?' said the young man.

'I gather she's marrying again after seven years of being her own woman, as she so prettily put it. Darling's in for a thin time, I'm afraid.'

He paid for the cigarettes, pocketed the change and walked back down the First Class corridor, towards the Hippo and the bitch.

[4]

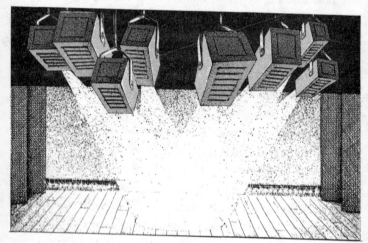

I Was
Adored Once Too

'In the beginning Birkett created the heaven and the earth,' said Birkett. 'And the earth was without form, and void; and darkness was upon the face of the deep.'

'Geddonwithit, Birk,' shouted voices in the darkness, up on the stage and down in the auditorium. Someone fell over a chair.

Working blind, he clipped off a length of wire and threaded it into the fuse.

'And the Spirit of Birkett moved upon the face of the waters . . .' He snapped the fuse back into its socket and put his hand on the master switch. '. . . And Birkett said, Let there be light: and there was light.'

At once, all the lights; white light from the floats and the battens, rose-pink light and amber from the floods, and eight suns hanging in the void beyond the stage, four on each side of the hall.

'Not bad, not bad,' said Cosgrove, who was standing a few feet away and had heard everything that he said. 'Now let's see you make a man.'

Birkett leaned over the rail of his crow's-nest by the switchboard and looked round the edge of the curtain. Way below the white giants a red dwarf was approaching the footlights, surrounded by a nebula: Mr Anderson, head of English, with his everlasting fag and his chequered cheese-cutter pulled well down over his eyes to protect them from the glare.

What could they call him but Andy Capp? They called him Andy Capp.

Andy Capp came up to the edge of the stage and leaned across the floats, shielding himself from them by cupping his hands under his eyes and peering through the mask of black shadow like a seedy bandit.

'When Birkett has finished trying to blow his hand off, perhaps we can get on with the rehearsal?'

Birkett drew back from the edge of his cast-iron cradle and set his hands to the dimmer switches. His lighting plot was tacked up above them, secretively recorded in his own shorthand:

P36 l. 15 exit M. D1 down 5 D2 down 10 simul.
     l. 20 D2 down 0 D3/4 down 5 change spots to dim *here* 1/2/3/4.

The light came and went at his command. He was far less likely to blow off his hand than was Andy Capp himself. When Andy Capp came up on stage and stood at the foot of Birkett's vertical iron ladder, Birkett wanted nothing so much as to put his boot on Andy Capp's head and screw it down into the floor, as the English teacher screwed down his own boot on his fag ends.

Andy Capp knew this as well as Birkett did, and stayed on the other side of the footlights, within spitting distance of Birkett but safe; because Andy Capp was Sir and Birkett was in 5b, good for fiddling with the lights and little else.

Fiddling was the right word. Birkett played on his dimmers with the love and skill of a virtuoso violinist, making night and day, the greater light and the lesser, with the tenderest touch of his long and flexible fingers. The woodwork master, now Stage Manager, was well aware of this, which was why he had given Birkett the lighting plot instead of doing it himself. As far as Andy Capp was concerned, Birkett was marooned on top of his ladder because he could do less damage there than he could on-stage, mangling Shakespeare.

And he could mend a fuse in the dark.

Birkett consulted the plot and without looking, placed his unerring hands on the dimmers. His eye was on the stage where Cosgrove, a pillow stuffed under his sweater, was reeling from side to side, supposedly drunk. Cosgrove, when genuinely drunk, was nothing like this, but after the effects had worn off he never could remember what it had been like. Cosgrove's mates had sworn to have him tanked up on the night so as to get an authentic performance out of him.

'Listen, Cosgrove,' said Andy Capp. Birkett's hands froze on the dimmers. 'This is *Twelfth Night*, not Saturday night at the Bricklayer's Arms. Sir Toby Belch is supposed to be tipsy in this scene, not paralytic.'

Cosgrove snapped upright and Howell, who was playing Sir Andrew Aguecheek, was knocked flying by the cushion. He went spinning across the stage, stiff-legged, like dividers across a map.

'Aguecheek,' said Andy Capp, 'is a foolish knight, not a berserk ballerina. Keep your twinkle toes on the ground. Get on with it, rabble.' His eyes slid upwards and sideways. Birkett knew that Andy Capp had something offensive ready to say to him as well, but there was no occasion to say it. Sir Toby and Sir Andrew faced each other; Sir Andrew's mouth opened and the dimmers began to move.

'Before me, she's a good wench,' said Sir Andrew.

'She's a beagle, true-bred, and one that adores me; what o' that?'

Sir Andrew raised his eyebrows. 'I was adored once, too.'

'Howell! Don't sound so bloody chatty,' Andy Capp bellowed from the darkness. 'That's one of your better lines. Make something of it. Like this.' He minced about beyond the footlights, now in focus, now out. '*I* was adored once *too*.'

'Oh, ducky,' murmured Cosgrove, out of the corner of his mouth.

'Get a laugh there,' said Andy Capp. 'It's the last one you'll get in this scene. And Birkett, keep your hot little hands off those dimmers. Are you trying to black us out?' Birkett let his hands drop. He had planned to make the light turn cold on that line, dimming out the amber and the rose, leaving only the white and blue battens. He had not bargained for a laugh; it didn't strike him as funny. There was a character in the play known as the Clown, but he was a wise guy, a professional fool. Aguecheek was the real fool.

'*I* was adored once *too*,' said Howell, flimsy-wristed, gyrating on pleated ankles. He had tucked his trousers into his socks to make himself feel Elizabethan. There was an immediate laugh from the resting actors, out of sight in the dark hall.

'Again!' cried Andy Capp.

'*I* was adored once *too*.'

There were two more scenes before the end of the act. On the stage below the players strutted, and at the switchboard above Birkett lightened their darkness and darkened their days. He felt as remote as God, operating the firmament; whatever was going on down there had nothing to do with him. The pain and the pleasure were outside his influence and he felt them only in terms of the coloured filters required to light each scene: blue and green for sorrow, pink and gold for joy, so that when he looked at the brilliant aquarium that was the stage he saw chaos. People hid behind hedges, assumed false names, slipped into disguises and climbed out of them. Lesley Pascoe, smooth and slender, golden girl of the High School, was cast as Viola, identical twin to Sebastian, and Sebastian was played by swarthy Noddy Newton who was so covered with thick black hair that when he tried on his costume it sprouted through the legs of his tights like winter wheat after a wet autumn.

All the female roles were being played by girls borrowed from the High School. As well as the three principals a number of friends turned up at each rehearsal to understudy or provide moral support in case anyone got jumped on in a dark cloakroom. Birkett knew none of them. They were the girls who went round with the boys who were down there on the stage; none of them people who would go round with Birkett.

It was nothing to do with him. He saw it and heard it and was out of it; even so, the words stayed in his mind, like dust caught in a net curtain. In the same way, and without wanting to, he had memorized the Bible. For years he had been a regular worshipper, with his parents, at the green tin chapel behind the bus station. One Sunday he had suddenly realized that he was no longer worshipping and after a month or two he stopped going there, but the damage was done already. It was widely believed that Birkett had sold his soul to the chapel and was stricken unable to enjoy himself, drink beer or think about women. People half expected him to turn up on the doorstep with leaflets, at inconvenient moments.

He looked down from the switchboard, one of them, but not one with them.

'To the gates of Tartar, thou most excellent devil of wit!' Sir Toby shouted. He strode off-stage and made a mock run up the ladder, repelled suddenly by the impact of his cushion against the rungs.

'And I'll make one too,' said Sir Andrew Aguecheek, with total irrelevance, as it seemed to Birkett. He wandered off in the other direction. Cosgrove's spotty brother, who was prompter and Assistant Stage Manager, swung on the knotted rope that dangled beside his chair. The curtains closed on Birkett's sunlit stage and Act Two was over. Cosgrove poked the cushion out of his sweater and looked up at Birkett.

'Don't you get struck by lightning for blasphemy?'

'Blasphemy?'

'Smitten with a plague of frogs?'

'Blasphemy?'

'Taking credit for the Universe,' said Cosgrove, but because Birkett had nothing laughable to say he lost interest and slid between the curtains, sylph-slim without his stomach which he left on-stage. He disappeared into the dark hall, followed by Howell.

'House lights!' Andy Capp was bawling. 'House lights, Birkett wake up for God's sake Birkett wake up Birkett . . .'

Howell put his head between the curtains again. 'Fiat lux, laddie. Fiat lux.' Howell knew Latin. Birkett didn't. The house lights were not his concern anyway; the switches were at the back of the hall, next to the wall bars. Finally someone remembered this and the lights were put on. Andy Capp's monotonous yelling subsided and cheerful conversation swelled up to fill the gap where it had been. Cups rattled. The girls who were not on-stage had made themselves responsible for serving drinks (although no one had dared ask them to) which they prepared in the Sixth Form Common Room and brought to the hall on trays. The spotty brother and other backstage personnel went through the curtains for coffee and fodder. Birkett stayed at the switchboard, setting up his lights for the next act. It was the same scene, but a different time of day:

Olivia's Garden. Full battens white 1/2 dim 0 blue 3. Amber floods full floats. 1/2/3/4 spots up full 5/6 down 8.

He made morning.

Number six dimmer was grating in its runner. Knowing that he had a quarter of an hour before Andy Capp drove the cast back to work Birkett took out a screwdriver and began to remove the casing. He first put up the master switch and worked in darkness, only his careful hands illuminated by the meagre glow from a badly shuttered window in the changing room behind him. In the corner of his eye he saw a narrow light spread across the stage and ebb again as someone opened the curtains and slipped through. Finished with the dimmer he replaced the casing and threw the master switch. There came an angry squeak from the foot of the ladder.

'Ow. Now you've made me spill it.'

One of the girls was standing there, clasping a thick china cup of slopped coffee. Birkett leaned over the rail.

'Was that my fault?'

'You made me jump, putting all the lights on like that.' She squinted up at him. He looked at the coffee cup.

'You haven't lost much. There's plenty left.'

'It isn't mine.'

'There's no one else here,' said Birkett.

'You're here.'

'Is it for me?' Nobody had brought him coffee before. There was no reason why he should not join the others in the hall, but apart from wanting a drink there was no reason why he should. He preferred to do without the drink.

'I suppose it must be,' she said. 'I was handing it out

[64]

and Tony Cosgrove said, "Don't forget God, back there,"
so I brought it through. Do they call you God?'

'They call me Birk,' said Birkett.

'Well, do you want the coffee or don't you, Birk?' said
the girl. 'I'm not going to call you that,' she said crossly.
'What's your real name?'

'Reuben,' said Birkett, reluctantly. The Twelve Tribes
of Israel were highly thought of at the tin chapel. He
disliked admitting to Reuben, but he had no second name. It
could have been worse. It could have been Zebulun. Or Gad.

'I'm Juliet.' She offered him the coffee, but when he
made no move to take it she withdrew her hand. 'Call me
Julie. Can I come up?'

'Juliet will do.' It didn't occur to him that one could
suffer as much from Juliet as from Reuben. 'You can come
up if you like.'

She stood on tiptoe and placed the cup on the floor of
the cradle. It was difficult for her to stand more on tiptoe
than she did already: her wedge heels were very high.

'You'd better take your shoes off,' he advised. She looked
suspicious, as if he had made an improper suggestion and
her friends had warned her about people like him, but she
came up the ladder, her lumpy heels going glamp glamp
glamp as they struck the iron rungs.

'You are a bit like God, so high up,' she said, leaning
against the rail. Birkett, pressed for space, had to turn
round with extreme care in case she thought he was making
advances.

'Turn the lights off again,' she said.

Now who's making advances? he wondered, as the darkness crashed down.

'It's snug up here.'

'About as snug as an oil rig.' Now that it was entirely dark he was aware of the draught from the changing-room window and the smell of old lunches that never quite died because the stage had once been used as a canteen, before the new one was built. The hot lights seemed to revive it. He pulled the switch again and Juliet stood blinking beside him.

'Birkett, stop b—ing about with those lights,' shouted Andy Capp, mindful that there were ladies present.

'Aren't you going to drink your coffee?' said Juliet. Birkett stepped forward to pick up the cup and managed to kick it over the edge of the cradle. It didn't break, but a greyer stain spread over the grey stage cloth.

'I'm always doing things like that,' he said.

'I was beginning to think you never did anything,' said Juliet, and went glamping down the ladder again. He put his head under the lower rail and watched her go.

'Are you in the play?' he said. 'I've never seen you onstage.'

'I'm a servant. Page sixty, Act Three, Scene Four, don't blink or you'll miss me.' He didn't say that he thought she was wasted as a servant. 'I'm understudying Maria, too.'

'That's the maid, isn't it?'

'It's the best part,' she said, quickly.

'I thought Lesley Pascoe . . .'

'Oh, Viola. That's nothing much. Maria's got the best lines of all the women. And she's funny,' said Juliet. She went towards the curtains with the empty cup. 'It's the best part . . . but you wouldn't know,' she said, and vanished.

She was right. He didn't know.

That night he read the play right through for the first time, and he was surprised to discover how much of it he knew already. He agreed that Maria was the best of the women's parts, but he doubted that Juliet would make much of a showing in it. Maria was a stinger; little, quick-witted, malicious. He thought of Juliet's large hopeful face and pile-driver legs.

On Thursday evening, when they stopped for a break, there was Juliet coming up the ladder glamp glamp glamp with two cups of coffee and a KitKat. His half of the Kit-Kat played merry hell with his demon back tooth, but he suffered in silence, showing her how the dimmers worked and explaining the runic mysteries of his lighting plot.

'Do you manage all this by yourself? I wouldn't have thought you'd have enough hands.'

He spread his fingers across the board and moved all eight dimmers at once.

'Like a pianist,' Juliet said. 'Stretching octaves. What about if you need to turn something else on, at the same time?'

'I use my nose. No, I *do*. In the mad scene where Mal-
volio thinks he's in the nut-house: I turn off this switch
here with my nose. Like this.'

'Well, it's long enough.' Juliet didn't seem to think that
it was a very nice accomplishment. 'You need Tony Cosgrove up here. He's all hands.'

'He'd be no good,' said Birkett. 'He'd be talking all the
time. You have to pay attention.'

'There's no one to talk to.'

'There would be if Cosgrove was here.'

At the end of the break Juliet remained at the top of the
ladder.

'You don't mind if I stay?'

'Of course not.' He should have said Oh please, do. In
fact, he did mind. The cradle was built to take at most two
people, both working. There was no room for ballast. Birkett was used to availing himself of the whole area and the
need to tread carefully spoiled his concentration. For the
first time he missed a lighting cue and was rewarded by a
blast of scorching scorn from Andy Capp, who happened
to notice, for once. The sympathetic touch of Juliet's hand
on his arm was no reward, and no consolation, either.

Cosgrove, bleary and becushioned, leered at him, one
finger laid to the side of his nose.

'Nudge, nudge, wink wink,' said Cosgrove, when he
came off-stage at the end of the scene and Birkett was
embarrassed in the dark; but at the same time mildly grati-
fied that Cosgrove imagined him to be having his evil way

– as Cosgrove certainly would have been, in his place.

At the next rehearsal Juliet was up there before him.

'Aren't you on in this scene?'

'Fancy you noticing.'

'I read the play.' He had read it again since last week. He was beginning to admire the way it was put together; two quite different stories spliced like cords, ending in a neat knot, but he didn't find it very funny and parts of it struck him as miserably cruel. He had always regarded Shakespeare as an effete twit who couldn't write a straight sentence to save his life, but he was beginning to see that Shakespeare might have got along very well with Andy Capp.

'Another bride, another groom, another sunny hu-hunnymoon,' sang Cosgrove at the foot of the ladder. 'Make with the sunshine, Birk.'

Juliet was picking her way through the lighting plot.

'I don't expect anyone but us understands this,' she said happily, building an intimate secret where there was neither secret nor intimacy. 'I'm not on-stage until here, look. I can run round the back, just before.'

And she did: and as soon as her little part was done she ran back again. Birkett did not hear her coming up the ladder. She had taken her shoes off.

'Don't you want to go for coffee?' said Birkett, when the break came.

'I asked Lesley to bring us some.' He guessed why she had asked Lesley when Lesley came through the curtains with a sulky shove, carrying a cup in either hand.

'Too busy to fetch your own?'

Juliet smiled a little, and then laughed, because the light was too dim for the smile to show. Birkett waited until Lesley had gone before sitting down to drink his coffee.

'It's a good thing we aren't fat,' said Juliet.

'Eh?'

'There's not much room up here.'

'We could always sit on the stage.' He stood up to consult the plot.

'Hey, Roo.' He supposed that it was short for Reuben.

'Yes?'

'I'm glad I'm not Viola.'

'You're even less like Noddy than Lesley is.'

'That's not what I meant. She's on-stage, all through the play.'

'Not all the time.'

'No, but on-off-on-off. It's the same with Maria. Suzanne's playing Maria. Do you know Suzanne? She's all sweaty by the end of the evening, from rushing about.'

'Dodging Cosgrove?'

'And that. I used to wish she'd be ill for a bit so that I'd get a chance at Maria; tonsillitis or something. She's got terrible tonsils, all her family have. When she turns her head you can see great lumps in her neck – just here.' She put her cool hand on his throat.

'I've had mine out,' said Birkett.

'I don't wish that any more.'

'Wish what?'

'That Suzanne would get tonsillitis. I'd sooner be here than on-stage.'

'Well, I wouldn't wish anyone had tonsillitis,' said Birkett. 'Except Andy Capp, maybe. It might shut him up.'

'Roo, why do you call him Andy Capp?'

'Oh God, look at him,' said Birkett. 'All he needs is a pigeon on his head.'

'What's his wife like? Florrie?'

'More like the Statue of Liberty. No, really. He hardly comes up to her chin.'

'Have they got any children?'

'Three.'

'I like children,' said Juliet. 'I'd like a lot of children.'

There was only one week left before opening night. In front of the curtain the stage had been extended by building it up with prefabricated blocks. Andy Capp called it the apron.

When the third act ended, Howell climbed over the apron and came through the curtains with the coffee. Juliet arranged for it to be delivered by a different person each time, and Birkett no longer wondered why.

'Working overtime, Birk?' said Howell. He stood on the bottom rung of the ladder and rested his chin on the top, level with their feet.

'Push off, Face-ache,' said Birkett.

'Aguecheek – Agueface – Face-ache; good thinking, Batman,' said Howell, sinking from sight. He reappeared a moment later, meandering across the stage in his Aguecheek walk, knees together, toes apart.

'You missed your cue again, in Scene Four,' said Howell. 'Do you know what Andy Capp said? "Bloody Birkett, busy with his skirt."'

'He never said that.' Beside him Juliet gave a little gasp, intending to sound outraged; only sounding pleased.

'It was said though,' said Howell. 'Your Birk-type secret is out, Birk.' He sprang backwards between the curtains. Nemesis got him. Someone had removed the block in the middle of the apron, and Birkett heard the crunch as he hit the floor.

'He's broken his leg; in two places. Should have been his neck,' said Andy Capp. 'He's in traction. Silly b—.' There were ladies present.

'What about my bruvver?' said Cosgrove. 'He's been prompter ever since we started. He knows the whole thing right through.'

'He couldn't play Aguecheek.'

'He could probably play Viola if you twisted his arm.'

'God forbid,' said Andy Capp. 'Anyway, we're not having him on-stage. Remember the carol concert?'

'Someone else knows it by heart,' said Cosgrove. He silently indicated the switchboard with his thumb. 'He remembers everything. He knows half the Bible for a start.'

'Birkett? He can't put one foot in front of the other without falling over.'

'Who'd notice? He's a dead ringer for Aguecheek,' said Cosgrove. 'You wouldn't even have to make him up.'

'Birkett! Get down here,' Andy Capp shouted. 'If you can spare the time,' he added, for the benefit of the cast. Birkett climbed down the ladder and approached the group in the middle of the stage.

'Good of you to drop in,' said Andy Capp. 'I'm sure you've got more interesting things to do. Cosgrove here says you're a quick study.'

'A what?'

'A quick study, har har,' said Andy Capp. 'He says you learn things easily.'

'Not me,' said Birkett.

'He thinks you know the whole play.'

'Not me.'

'Come off it,' said Cosgrove. 'You've been sitting up there watching us for the past six months. You must know it.'

Birkett guessed what they were after.

'Not me.'

'Not I,' said Andy Capp.

Cosgrove put on his cushion and his Sir Toby voice and said sharply. 'Did she see thee the while, old boy? tell me that.'

'As plain as I see you now,' said Birkett, without thinking.

'Art thou good at these kick-shaws, knight?'

'As any man in Illyria, whatsoever he be, under the degree of my betters; and yet I will not compare with an old man,' said Birkett.

'She's a beagle, true-bred, and one that adores me; what o' that?'

'*I* was adored once *too*.'

'Beat that,' said Cosgrove.

Andy Capp thrust a book into Birkett's hands. 'There you are, Aguecheek. Get on with it.'

'But I don't understand it all.'

'Then you'll have a lot in common with the audience,' said Andy Capp. 'You have a week. Get on with it.'

'Who'll do the lights?' said Birkett. 'I'm the only one who knows the plot.'

'Damn the lights. What's the good of lights if we have no play?' said Andy Capp. 'Leave 'em all switched on. Come on, rabble. Act One, Scene Three.'

The rehearsal got under way. Birkett held the book in his hands and never looked at it once. When it was his turn to speak he spoke, helplessly, the very words that Howell had spoken, and in the very tone that Howell had spoken them.

'Proper polly parrot, aren't you?' muttered Cosgrove, when he stumbled on his lines and Birkett prompted him, still without looking at the book. 'You taking English "A" level, next year?'

'You're joking.'

'Do it. You'll have a walk-over.'

At the end of the scene Birkett ran from the stage and made for the ladder, hoping that he would have time to get up there and adjust the lights before he was wanted, but as he put his hands to the rungs the floods came on and the dimmers went up. Juliet looked over the railing.

'Don't worry about me, Roo. I can manage.'

He hadn't been worrying about her. He had forgotten that she was there.

'I told you I could understand it.'

'Better leave it,' said Birkett, furious at finding his true place usurped. 'I've made alterations – you won't be able to follow them.'

'I know your writing,' said Juliet, comfortably. 'Go back on-stage. You're doing ever so well. I didn't know you were so good.'

'I'm not,' he growled, and thought it was true. He was a proper polly parrot.

'You, Birkett, are a double-dyed creep,' said Andy Capp, leaning across the apron. 'Is this the case that dropped a thousand bricks? Is this the celebrated numb-skull who has forgotten to hand in his homework six weeks out of nine? Well, we've found you out now, you twister.'

'Polly parrot,' said Birkett, under his breath.

'Get on with it, rabble.'

They got on with it, and Juliet got on with the lights. Birkett knew to the second when a change was due, and to the second the changes were made. He made a note to dim number two spot when he had the chance. It shone straight in his eye every time he faced right.

'Excellent,' Sir Toby roared in his ear. 'I smell a device.'

'I have't in my nose too,' said Birkett, in a reedy nasal whine, out-Howelling Howell. A happy laugh surged out of the darkness.

Sir Toby roared longer and louder, piqued that Birkett was getting bigger laughs than he was.

'My purpose is indeed a horse of that colour,' said Maria, arching her long neck like a thoroughbred. Birkett could see no sign of swollen tonsils.

'And your horse would now make him an ass,' he said, and was half drowned by another high tide of laughter. They were laughing at him, not with him, but he supposed that that was what he was there for.

Maria spoke again and went out, blowing kisses to Sir Toby.

'Good night, Penthesilia,' said Sir Toby.

'Before me, she's a good wench,' said Birkett.

'She's a beagle, true-bred, and one that adores me; what o' that?'

'*I* was adored once *too*.' The laughter exploded all round him as he stood there, a dead ringer for Sir Andrew Aguecheek; lank yellow hair drooping over his white face, round eyes staring, long arms dangling. What a thought; Birkett; adored; har har, as Andy Capp would say.

Suddenly the lights turned blue, stuttered, went dim, became bright again, went out entirely and then came on in a frightful blaze, all eight suns burning him alive.

'What the hell is going on?' demanded Andy Capp, vaulting on to the apron like a galvanized leprechaun and hurling his copy of the play across the stage. 'Who did that?'

Birkett turned to the switchboard in a rage.

'You silly cow! Leave it alone. I altered that bit. I said you wouldn't understand it.'

'Who's up there? Who is it? Come down here, now,' said Andy Capp, more terrible in a whisper than he ever was at full volume.

Juliet came down the ladder glamp glamp glamp on her club heels and stumbled towards them. Her face was a brighter pink than any floodlight could have made it, and her eyes were enormous with tears.

'I thought . . .'

'Thought?' Andy Capp was incredulous. 'Who asked you to think? Who asked you to touch the switchboard? It's a skilled job, not a game for silly little girls.'

Juliet moved towards Birkett. Birkett moved away.

'I told you,' he said.

'I thought I knew it,' said Juliet. She bent her head and the tears fell to the floor. They made greyer spots on the grey stage cloth. 'I thought I had it right. I'm always up there.'

'Don't we know it? And we know why: you made sure of

that,' said Andy Capp, unforgiveably. 'Now get off the stage and get out of the way, there's a good girl. Do your courting out of school, next time.'

Juliet tried to look at Birkett. Birkett looked up at the proscenium arch. The second amber flood was dead. He thought there might be a spare bulb in the box below the switchboard. If not, he would have to get one ordered tomorrow. When he looked round again, Juliet was gone, climbing awkwardly over the apron and down into the hall. The darkness took her. Andy Capp followed.

'Get on with it, rabble.'

'Good night, Penthesilia,' said Sir Toby.

'Before me, she's a good wench.'

'She's a beagle, true-bred, and one that adores me; what o' that?'

'I was adored once too,' said Birkett.

[5]

Enough is Too Much Already

'Look,' Maurice said, 'lay off, will you? I've told you I'm sorry, haven't I? I mean, I *mean* it. I *am* sorry.'

'You look it,' Nazzer said. 'You look so sorry my heart bleeds for you. Doesn't he look sorry?' said Nazzer, turning to Nina for confirmation. 'Tears pouring down his little face.'

'We waited outside for *half an hour*,' Nina said. 'It was freezing. Real brass monkeys. Cardy says she's not interested any more. We only *asked* her because you said you fancied her. Now she thinks I've been sending her up. Cardy's my best friend,' Nina said. 'Was.'

'If you'd been in my position,' Maurice began.

'Catch me in any position you'd be in,' said Nina. 'Next time you get your eye on a girl, you do your own fishing.'

'I'm not making excuses,' said Maurice. 'I've got a *reason*. I was unavoidably delayed. Nah, *shut* up, Nina, I'm trying to tell you. You know I nearly missed the train last night –'

'How should I know?'

'Because it was you kept me hanging about trying to set me up for Cardy –'

'I like that! You were the one –'

'I only suggested that she might like –'

'The way you go on anyone would think they were forming queues –'

'If you'll only listen,' Maurice said.

'I mean, you think you look so *glorious* –'

'Lady, give the guy a chance,' Nazzer pleaded. 'Turn down the goddam *volume*, willya?'

'Well I *did*.'

'What?'

'Nearly miss the train. It was about twenty-five past when I got to the station, and I'm just running on to the platform when old Patterson looms up like King Kong, out of a rubbish bin. I reckon he was trying to fish out the *Sun* while no one was looking. "Ho, Nicholls," he says, "didn't we have a little appointment at lunchtime?" and we had had, only I'd forgotten, and I said, "I can't stop now, Sir. I'll miss me train," and *he* started saying something, and the geezer on the public address started bawling something about a platform change, and would we all please pay attention, so I couldn't hear a word anyway –'

'*No*body can hear a word old Patterson says,' Nazzer remarked.

'– and old Patterson's still going on, so I just said, "Yes Sir, sorry Sir," and ran like hell and jumped on the train.'

'I heard,' Nina said. 'You don't have to tell me. It was on the News, this morning. *Maurice Nicholls caught his train. Norwich rocked to its foundations.* Right before the earthquake in China, it was. And the Third World War breaking out.'

'Well, it looked all right, and I sat down, and got my physics out, like I was meant to have given Patterson at dinner-time, when this girl gets on.'

'I hope you don't think I'm going to tell Cardy all this?' Nina said. 'I mean, this is going to make her feel really marvellous, isn't it?'

'No, give it a rest,' Maurice said. 'I didn't really see her at first. I just noticed these legs going by.'

'Oh. Legs,' Nazzer murmured, into his coffee. 'Legs.'

'*Not* what you think, Naz. You got a scaly mind. She was wearing those horrible wrinkly leg-warmers that look like lagging on old water pipes,' Maurice said.

'Thanks a million,' Nina said, peering under the table and adjusting something through her skirt.

'And anyway, she goes and stands up the front with all the other Red Berets –'

'Oh, a St Ursula's Virgin,' said Nazzer. 'Legs . . .'

'They *all* wear those short leg-warmers that only come up to your knees,' Nina said. 'It's some soft sort of fashion, or something. They *always* fall down.'

'– and she starts chatting to them, and then I see Langham up front, too.'

'Langham doesn't go on your train.'

'That's what I thought, and I'm just about to go up and say, "Get your great greasy body off our train, Langham," when he gets up for something, and she steps back and treads on his foot.'

'Yes?'

'What?'

'What happened?'

'Nothing happened,' Nazzer droned. 'You could drop a breeze-block on Langham's foot and he wouldn't notice. You could drop a breeze-block on his *head* –'

'He noticed, all right. He lets out this great horrible roar – you know, that sort of *Wrrroagh!* noise you get at First Division matches, and she turns round and says, "Oh, I'm sorry. Did I hurt you?" She had a nice voice,' Maurice reported, mournfully.

'And Langham starts mincing about and flapping his hands and squeaking, "Ooooh, Ai'm sorreigh. Did Ai hurt yaw?" and then the train starts – you know how those little pay trains jolt when they start –'

'They're only buses on rails,' Nazzer said. 'If they did away with the bridges they could have double-decker pay trains.'

'– and she falls against him, and he yells, "Oh, oh, she's after me, look, she fancies me, ooh-ooh-ooh!" and starts pulling her about, and she gives him a shove, and I can see him getting nasty –'

'*Getting?*' Nina said. 'He's a fat horrible pig, that Langham.'

'Well, I thought, someone'll stop it, but all the old geezers thought it was just kids mucking about, and let him get on with it. You know, she was really upset; you could see that, but they just went on reading the paper and looking out of the windows. I could just imagine them all sitting and watching a murder, like it was something on telly, and not doing anything about it.'

'What about the other Virgins?'

'Oh, I thought *they'd* do something, you know, I mean . . . there were *six* of them, but they just giggled a bit and looked the other way, and one of them said, "Some people'll do *anything* to get a bit of attention," and someone else says, "Oh, *her*," real snarky. And she tried to pull away from him, but he got her by the strap of her bag –'

'This is getting really exciting,' said Nina. 'Isn't it, Naz? Don't you wish you could stay for the end?'

'It wasn't funny. You wouldn't have thought it was funny if it had been you. She had the strap wrapped round her wrist, and he kept twisting it – you know what a great lunk he is, Naz –'

'Why do people keep asking *me*?' said Nazzer.

'You pulled out of the Second Eleven because of Langham,' Maurice said. 'And this Cilla was only a small little thing.'

'Oh; *Cilla*, was it?'

'You know her?'

'No, but I mean – *Cilla*.'

' 'Sno dafter than Nina,' Nazzer said morosely, inspecting the bottom of his cup.

'I don't know how you've lived so long, Nazzer –'

'She was starting to cry, and the train was shaking around all over the points, and she nearly fell on me –'

'She seems to fall on a lot of people, this Cilla,' Nina remarked.

'So I got up and tapped Langham on the back of the neck –'

'Langham hasn't got a neck,' Nazzer said. 'His head grows out of his deltoids.'

'Watch your language,' Nina said.

'– with the edge of my physics book, and I said, "Lay off, Langham," and he looks at me and says, "You're going the long way home, aren't you?" I thought he was being cryptic, meaning, *I'm going to duff you up, shortly*, but I said, "Lay off, Langham, will you, or I shall have to rearrange you," and *he* said, "You and whose army?" '

'He would,' Nazzer said. 'I've never heard him come

out with *anything* original; I don't reckon he *was* being cryptic, you know. He's not really programmed for it.'

'So I got my physics book and hit him behind the left knee.'

'Why the left knee?'

'He couldn't reach any higher,' Nazzer explained.

'The left knee is a vulnerable spot on Langham, right now,' Maurice said, 'since Saturday's match. You know what it's like, first match of the Autumn Term. There was a lot of old scores settled on Saturday; sort of backlog left over from Easter. Someone reckoned up with Langham's left leg. Anyway, it worked. He went over backwards, sort of Z-shaped. I wish you could have seen him, Naz. It would have made up for a lot.'

'I'll think about it in Maths,' Nazzer said. 'It'll cheer me up no end.'

'So I said to this girl, this Cilla, "Come on, let's get down the other end," and she said, "Supposing he follows us?" so I said, "I can always pull the emergency chain." '

'That's what Superman does, you know,' said Nazzer. 'When Lois Lane's in peril, he flies to the rescue and pulls the emergency chain. And the emergency bog flushes,' he added.

'I was *joking*,' Maurice said, heavily. 'So anyway, we sort of stepped over Langham, and all these old geezers and ladies were sucking their false choppers, and old Langham was groaning, and this Cilla, she looks at me like I *was* Superman. I mean, it wasn't bad going, was it? I mean, it *was* Langham, and I did *thump* him.'

'What did the Virgins do?'

'Nothing. But they looked a bit envious,' Maurice conceded, modestly.

'He's not at school today,' Nina said.

'Maybe you killed him,' said Nazzer.

'Well, he *didn't* come after us, did he?' Maurice said. 'He couldn't. No, I didn't kill him. I saw him get off at Brundall. He was limping.'

'Brundall?'

'He lives at Brundall.'

'But you were on the Sheringham train.'

'Well, that's it, you see,' Maurice said. 'We weren't. We just arrived at the back end of the train, when we got to the place where the Sheringham line branches off, and I noticed we weren't on it. I mean, the track had branched off, but the train was still on the Yarmouth line.'

'So that's where you were,' Nina said. 'Yarmouth! I'm not telling Cardy. You'd better think of something better, or something.'

'No! It wasn't like that. See, I realized then that I'd got on the wrong train, so I thought, well, I'll get off at Brundall, then I thought, no I won't, that's where Langham gets off – I'll get off at Buckenham. And so we get to Brundall and I see old Langham falling about on the platform – you *would* have enjoyed it, Naz – and then the conductor comes along, and I realized I'd only got my season to Worstead, and it's not even *on* that line, and this girl, this Cilla, she's still sitting next to me, sniffing, and I don't know where she's getting off, and I don't want to lose sight of her yet. So anyway, the conductor gets to us, and I say, politely, "You first," and she hums and hahs a bit, and the conductor says, "Where to, darling?" and in the end she says, "Reedham," and she blushes a bit, and says, "I don't really live there. I'm just going to see someone."

'He gives her a ticket.

'I say, "Can I come with you?" and she giggles and says, "Better not; it's my auntie."

' "And what about you?" says the conductor, to me.

'Well, I was stuck, wasn't I? I mean, we were just coming in to Buckenham, but I *couldn't* get off before she did. I didn't know her name or where she lived, or anything.'

'I thought you said her name was Cilla,' Nina snapped.

'Yes, but I didn't know that yet, did I? I had to find out, didn't I? And I ask you; Reedham! It's like the end of the world. And I said, "Berney Arms," because that's the next station after Reedham, and he says, "This train don't go to Berney Arms. This is the Lowestoft train." '

'I thought you said it was going to Yarmouth,' Nina said.

'It's the same line, till Reedham,' Maurice said. 'So I looked a right nutter, didn't I, and I said, "Oh, then I'll go on to Haddiscoe and borrow me brother-in-law's bike," so he gives me a ticket.'

'Your brother-in-law's out on the rigs, isn't he?' Nazzer said.

'His bike isn't.'

'No, his bike's in the garage down Earlham Road,' said Nina.

'The conductor didn't know that, did he?' Maurice said. 'Look, I was *lying*, for God's sake. I just wanted to find out a bit more about her. That's natural, isn't it?'

'If you say so.'

'I s'pose you'd forgot about us,' Nina said.

'Well . . . it was only ten to five, then. I hadn't even *started* thinking about you. So we got talking, and she says she's only just started at St Ursula's, and her name's Cilla Hales, and she lives in Wymondham, and I think that's brilliant, because the Wymondham train goes at five-twenty, so I can see her every evening, and then get the six o'clock home. Then we stop at Cantley, and all the other Virgins get out – what d'you think so many of them could be doing in Cantley? They can't all be Catholics out there –'

'There's nothing else to do,' Nazzer said, 'except the beet refinery, but that doesn't open till Monday.'

'Anyway, they all get out, and Cilla ducks her head down and says, "Stupid stuck-up cows," and then we talked a bit, and we're nearly at Reedham, and she's getting ready to go. So I say, "I'll see you tomorrow, shall I?" and she says, "Oh yes. Thanks ever so for – you know what," and I say, "Well, it was nothing. Let's meet in the buffet for coffee," and she says, "OK, let's," and then we're in Reedham.

'So, she got off, and waved at me from the platform as the train moved off. I hoped her auntie was meeting her, because the mist was coming down really thick. Oh God, it's like the end of the world, Reedham, it's like the end of the Universe.'

'End of the Universe's a time, not a place,' Nazzer said.

'Time and Place are the same thing,' Nina said. 'Old Patterson told us.'

'That's Time and *Space*.'

'It's right on the edge of the marshes –'

'What is?'

'Reedham.'

'I know,' Nazzer said. 'My mum took me there for a picnic when I was a young lad. I fell in a dyke and nearly drowned.'

'Are you sure they got you out in time?' Nina said. 'Brain death can occur after four minutes. I mean, you might have got left under for five.'

'Brain *damage*, not brain death,' Nazzer said. 'Brain death's when they pull the plug on your life-support system and break you up for spares.'

'– at least,' Maurice went on, 'I thought it was like the end of the world until we got to Haddiscoe. There's *nothing* at Haddiscoe, just two platforms. There's not even a bridge or a subway – you have to walk across the lines.'

'It's Doomsville, man.' Nazzer.

'Well, I got out of the train, I was the only one, and I stood and watched it going away into the mist – it was getting really thick by now, and I couldn't see anything, just the rear light on the train and a telephone box down the road. Well, I looked at the timetable and there's a train back from Lowestoft at thirty-three minutes past, so I ring me mum and say I won't be home for tea, and I go for a walk. In the mist. All on me tod.'

'Thinking about Cilla?' Nazzer played soulful music on an imaginary violin.

'Why not?' Maurice demanded. 'I'd done all right, hadn't I? And I was going to see her next day, so I thought it was worth getting stuck at Haddiscoe. I could hear this horrible noise, a sort of quiet tearing sound. It really frightened me, you know, it was all around. You couldn't see where it was coming from.'

'Don't think I've *ever* seen a noise,' Nina said.

'You ever been out in the garden at night and listened to the snails eating the lettuces? It was like that, only about a hundred times louder. Well, I walked around a bit, and went back to the station and waited, and the train didn't come and didn't come, and I thought they must have cancelled it. It was bloody cold, I can tell you, Naz – you'd never think it was only September.'

'We were cold too, weren't we, Naz?' Nina said.

'Anyway, it came in the end – I could hear it for ages before I could see it, and I got on.'

'What was the tearing noise?' Nazzer asked.

'Cows eating the grass,' Maurice said. 'They were all

over the place. I think they must go on eating all night, all the year round.

'Well, I sat on the train, and it was *crawling* along, because of the mist, and I was perishing cold, but I didn't really mind – I was thinking about Cilla. And then the train stopped at Reedham, and the door opened, and there she was.'

'Who?'

'Lois Lane,' said Nazzer.

'Cilla. Her. She came and sat down right opposite me and I thought, 'ere 'ere, and then she looked up and saw me. She went right pink – then green,' Maurice said.

'So I said, "That was a short visit, wasn't it?" and she said, "What happened to your brother-in-law's bike?" real snarky.

'And I said, "Wasn't your auntie in?" and she looked at me all funny and says, "Was your brother-in-law out?"

'And then she said, "You got straight back on the train, didn't you? You don't live round here at all, do you? Not even at Berney Arms," and I said, "No, well, actually I live at Worstead."

'She said, "Why were you going to Haddiscoe?"

'And I said, "I didn't want to get off the train before you did. I wanted to stay with you a bit longer," but it didn't work. She said, "But Worstead's on the other line," and I said, "I got on the wrong train." She said, "Well, why didn't you get off it?" and I said, "Like I said, I wanted to stay with you till you got out."

'And she said, "I was on the wrong train too. I only got on to give my mate a book and that fat fella jumped on me."

'And I said, "Well, I saved you, didn't I?" and she said, "You might have said something. We could have got off at Brundall and hitched back."

'And I said, "You mean, you stayed on the train because of me?"

'And she said, "You mean, you only stayed on because of me?" and I said "Yes."

'And she said, "Blast you! I've missed the Wymondham train and there isn't another till half-past eight."

'And I said, "Well, I can't get one till eight, either – that's nearly as bad. Let's have a coffee in the buffet at Norwich," and she said, "Bugger the buffet. My mum'll go spare when I get in," and she got up and went all the way to the other end of the train. I watched her, all the way.'

Nina said, 'Is that all?'

'*All?*' Maurice echoed. 'Isn't that *enough*?'

'Too much,' Nazzer murmured. 'Did you see her again?'

'In the distance,' Maurice said, 'and I saw her in the buffet at Norwich, but she wouldn't talk to me. When I sat down she got up and went to another table . . . So I followed her, and she got up and moved again, and I went over and said, "I don't know why you're so angry," and she said, "I suppose you think it's funny," and I said

"Yes," and she said, "That's why I'm angry," and got up and found *another* table. She kept on doing it. It was like musical chairs. In the end I went out and got my train – and then I found I'd left my school bag with my season and all on Haddiscoe Station. The cows have probably eaten it by now. My physics was in there too.

'Anyway, that's why I didn't come to the disco last night,' said Maurice.

[6]

Mrs Tulkinghorne's First Symphony

He woke briefly at five, when the sun rose, and saw the meadow between the house and the broad opaque with mist. When he himself rose, two hours later, the mist was slithering away between the elms, over the green and white hawthorn hedges; and through the last drifts of it, among the buttercups and lady's smocks, a woman was walking. At the edge of the broad he could see the blue plateau of a cabin-cruiser's roof.

There was no public right-of-way across the meadow from the broad. The approaching woman must have discovered the path that they had made for themselves although, like most local people, they never went out on to the water. It was the preserve of foreigners in hired boats, and at the height of the season, on a morning like this, would be as crowded as a city car park, with pleasure craft moored to the bank or anchored, farther out, on mud weights.

He could see her more clearly now, definite among the hazy flowers in a sharp white sun dress. He wondered where she was going, or where she thought she was going, and was mildly interested when she opened the gate in the hedge at the end of the garden and came up the path between the onion bed and the fruit cage. She walked slowly and gazed about her with seeming pleasure, before passing out of sight below the window sill. He heard the back door open.

When he went down to the kitchen his mother was returning from the rear lobby looking surprised and oddly amused with it.

'Who was the woman in white?' he asked.

'"O fat white woman whom nobody loves",' said his sister Frances, already at the table, pouring orange juice.

'I went to hang out the tea towels and she came up from the water like Undine,' his mother said, 'asking if we sold milk and eggs.'

'Why should we?' Frances said.

'Holiday-makers think that country people always sell milk and eggs, I suppose. She wasn't fat – not as fat as me, anyroad.'

'She must have heard Arthur's capons over the hedge,' Nicholas said. 'Eggs? She'll be lucky. What did you tell her? Wait till Prycewyse opens at nine?'

'Of course not. I didn't want to disappoint her.' His mother settled billowing into her chair, like a deflating helium balloon, and reached for the coffee jug. 'She didn't realize there are shops down the road. You know you can't see the village from the water when the mist's up; and our may hides Arthur's scrapheap at this time of year. She thought I was a nice stout farmer's wife coming out to feed the hens . . .'

'Oh really!' Frances's voice sharpened. 'She must have seen this isn't a working farm.'

'I doubt it. She looked rather dazzled . . . there was buttercup pollen on her skirt. Probably she didn't even want milk and eggs very much – just thought that on a May morning in a meadow that's what she ought to be wanting.'

Frances squinted suspiciously over the orange juice.

'So what *did* you tell her?' Out of the window Nicholas could see the woman in white meandering through the gold and silver of their back meadow.

'I said one of you would bring them down later.'

'How much later?' Nicholas asked. 'The milk won't

be here till eleven and I finished the eggs last night.'

'Jack won't mind *us* going to the back door early,' his mother said.

'You mean you pretended we sold milk and eggs?' Frances was incredulous. 'I suppose you think I'm going down there in a muslin dress and bare feet with straw in my hair? Well I can't. If I don't hurry I'll miss the bus. Nick can go.'

'*I'll* go by bus. You can borrow my bike,' he offered. He stood up.

'No dice. If Mum wants to play sun-fresh dew-picked farmers' wives with some batty boat person, let her. I'm not joining in.'

'What's eating her?' Nicholas asked, as the door slammed.

'We were having a full and frank exchange of ideas, before you came down.'

'A row.'

'She wants to move closer to Norwich,' said his mother. 'For choice she'd like to live in the bus station where all her friends hang out.'

'Norwich bus station is the only place in the world that smells of stale cigarette smoke outdoors,' Nicholas said. 'Except our garden.'

'I only smoke when I'm thinking,' his mother said, quickly. 'Now, go round to Jack's, will you? Ten eggs.'

'Milk?'

'We've got some to spare.'

'I bet your woman in white thinks that hens still lay eggs in dozens. She'll think that Jack's got a tally stick instead of a cash register that plays tunes.'

'She doesn't know about Jack. Move.'

He walked the hundred yards to Jack's supermarket, hidden by mist and mayflowers from the innocent eyes of the boat people on the broad, along with Arthur Hewitt's used car mart, the garage, the chippie, and the functional flanks of the houses on the council estate. The eggs came in a yellow polystyrene carton: FRESH it said on the side, as if there could be any doubt. When he returned to the house his mother was pouring milk from a bottle into a blue and white striped jug. She offered him a matching bowl for the eggs.

'You gone bananas?' he asked. 'Do you want me to run up to *Ikens* and borrow Mervyn's Morris bells?' He executed two or three lumpish hops from one foot to the other, arms flapping.

'You're as bad as Frances. There's no need to despise townies. They've got to live somewhere.'

'Yes, in weekend cottages that local people can't afford any more, like Mervyn the Morris man.'

'Like us?'

'At least we aren't weekenders. Catch Arthur or Jack with bells round their knees!'

'Spoken like a true local,' said his mother, waspishly. Born and raised in Leeds she could still understand the wonder of drifting through a water meadow towards a farmhouse that basked in the low morning sun of early summer. Nicholas had missed being born a townie by, as she vulgarly put it, the skin of his placenta. 'She's on holiday, for God's sake. She's in the heart of rural England. Let her see it as she thinks it is.'

'Protect her from the sight of Arthur's scrapheap, you mean? Would you buy a used car from this man? Lady, I wouldn't buy a *new* car from this man –'

'Get down to the boat, lad. Tell her she can bring the china back later.'

'She might pinch it.'

'She wouldn't cheat honest country folk. That's not part of the picture.'

'What honest country folk? Jack and Arthur?'

'*Shift.*'

His mother, in her long smock dress, moved with heavy purpose towards her work room. Nicholas walked down the garden and into the meadow, carrying in one hand the blue and white banded bowl of brown eggs, in the other the jug, its contents protected by a little mantilla of white net, with blue glass beads sewn round the edge. Behind him a voice called from an upper window:

> '"*In a somer season whan soft was the sonne,*
> *I shope me in shroudes as I a shepe were,*
> *In habite as an heremite unholy of workes,*
> *Went wide in this world wondres to here.*
> *Ac on a May morning . . .*"'

'Shut up, Ma!'

The air was already warmer than it had been when he went round to Jack's for the eggs, unexpectedly hot for the time of year. He'd known May mornings when hail had stripped the meadow of every petal and thrashed the surface of the broad like a sandblaster. Putting down his cargo among the buttercups he first loosened, then removed his black school tie. With the white shirt and black uniform trousers it made him feel like an undertaker's assistant.

As he approached the water's edge the cabin-cruiser, whose roof he had seen from his bedroom window, came into view again behind the rank cow parsley. Watching out for the crampons that pinned her to the bank, for fear of tripping on a mooring line, he came through the cow parsley to find himself looking down at the deckhead of a thirty-foot boat that rode like a great trustful duck in the shallow water. He read her name on the prow: *Irene Rose*.

Irene Rose had the water to herself. The broad was deserted from one side to the other, still as a dewpond. He heard a cuckoo echoing in the elms by the church, a brief clap of wings and water as a little mallard and her drake took to the air, and music: Mahler's First Symphony. It was coming from the boat. There was no sign of the woman in white. He called 'Hullo?' and unhooking one knuckle from the handle of the jug, stooped to tap on a window. No one came. Across the broad the cuckoo called, answered by Mahler's cuckoo in the cabin.

Balancing the eggs and milk with extreme care, he straddled the gap between bank and boat, and stepped down on to the deck. *Irene Rose*, newly painted white and blue, carried none of the insignia that would have identified her with a local boatyard. She must be privately owned and her owner seemed to have fallen overboard. Nicholas edged along the side of the cabin and looked down into the cockpit.

'Hullo!'

The door of the cabin opened and his customer stared out.

'Milk,' he said, offering first the jug, then the bowl. 'Eggs.'

The face below him relaxed into a smile.

'Oh, how lovely. Do come into the . . . the *galley*.' She seemed proud to know the right word. There were three steps down. It was a spacious craft, not new, but recently refurbished, and unlike a hired craft of the same size, its galley was quite separate from the cabin, fitted like a real landlocked kitchen. Even the blue butane canister was no more out of place than it would have been in a cottage scullery. At the far end an open doorway led into the cabin, and through it Mahler's cuckoo called and called.

'Like it?' said the woman in white.

'It's beautiful.' He did not know whether she meant the galley or the music. He gestured with bowl and jug. 'Where shall I put these?'

'Oh, there please.' She pointed to the working surface.

'*We* think she's rather special. We bought her in the autumn and spent the last nine months doing her up. My husband's retired – he's older than I am –'

Should I care? he thought.

'– so he's got plenty of spare time. I don't work. Come and see.'

He put down his groceries and followed her into the cabin. There was no evidence of the retired husband of advanced age. The woman, he judged, was older than his mother, perhaps fifty, but as trim as her boat in the white sun dress.

The cabin looked like a cottage parlour of historical fiction; chintz curtains, ornaments, little tables, even a chair. On a teak shelf below the windows stood a record deck. The woman gestured to it.

'Mahler.'

'Yes. First Symphony, first movement.'

She seemed delighted that he should know.

'Would you like some coffee?'

He knew he ought to refuse. He had left his watch on the bathroom window sill, but he guessed that it must be fast approaching the time when he should leave for school.

'John – my husband – went to see if he could get any diesel. He was afraid we'd run out before we could get to a – a what d'you call it, staithe. Will he find a garage, do you think?'

He could not resist telling her.

'About a hundred yards away, actually; past our place. You can't see the village from here.'

She laughed. 'Then he's certainly got lost. He's been gone over half an hour. He went down along the bank.'

'He'll be all right. There's a boat station at Ilstead, two miles down river.'

'Aren't we on a broad?'

'Yes, but the broad's on a river.'

'I don't know *anything* about this place. Do stay for coffee and tell me things.'

He stood in the doorway, watching her prepare it. He had expected a jar of Nescafé, but she had a complex filter arrangement laid out on the working surface. It was going to take a long time. He would certainly be late for school, but he was reluctant to leave the restful cabin, cool on the water that dappled the ceiling with reflections; reluctant to miss the chance of hearing Mahler without Frances yammering through the quiet parts, yelling to make herself heard above the louder passages, stamping and flouncing along with the crescendos. Least of all did he want to pass up the pleasure of real coffee prepared by a gracious woman in a white dress who begged for his company, in exchange for Assembly and a German class.

'It was so good of your mother to let me have the milk and eggs. John – my husband – said he'd try and bring some back, but when I went up on deck and saw your farm, I couldn't resist asking. I was dying to cross that meadow. How much do I owe you?'

He guessed wildly. 'A pound?'

She said, 'That's awfully generous for fresh produce.' He wondered what she would think when she tasted the thin Norfolk milk and hoped that she did not come from a dairy county.

She asked, pouring coffee, 'What's your name? I'm Margery Tulkinghorne.'

It was not a name that he could associate with any particular area, but it did not sound like Devon, where the earth was red, the grass was lush, and the cream lay like a golden cape on the shoulders of the milk.

'Nicholas Hinchcliffe.'

'A Yorkshireman.' She was clearly at the same game.

'No, born here.' By the skin of my placenta, actually. 'My parents are – were – from Yorkshire, I mean.'

They took their coffee to the cabin, in solid but elegant hand-thrown mugs. Nicholas sat in the spoon-backed chair that was fastened to the floor, making him feel as if he were tied down. Mrs Tulkinghorne sat on a divan. Mahler's second movement filled the little room.

'What's the name of the river?' Mrs Tulkinghorne asked.

'The Ant.'

'Really? Crossing Breydon Water we passed a boat called *River Ant*.' She laughed. 'I thought it was some kind of strange species.'

'Like Desert Rat?' He laughed too. They began to feel easier, he thought. The absent husband seemed more absent. The record ended.

'Shall we have the other side?' Mrs Tulkinghorne asked, rising, 'or would you like something different?'

His coffee was still too hot to drink; he was going to be very late for school. 'Something different, please.'

He was about to ask if she had the Fourth, as well, but Mrs Tulkinghorne was lifting the record from the turntable, spanning her hand from label to rim to avoid touching the grooves. She looked carefully at him. 'Let me guess what you'd like.'

Uncomfortably he shifted in the immovable chair.

'Prokofiev's "Classical"?'

'One of my favourites.'

'Mine too.'

She bent to find it in a cupboard beneath the shelf. He thought, How on earth can you know what I like? irritated because she *had* known. He said, 'Another first.'

She stood up, grasping it. 'What do you mean?'

'Another first symphony – like the Mahler.'

'I collect them.' She took it out of its sleeve, placed it on the turntable and lowered the arm.

'So do we. Mum gets the choral works and I pick the orchestral. My sister only buys pop. We don't count that.'

'I meant,' Mrs Tulkinghorne said, 'that I collect first symphonies.'

'What a good idea.' He smiled.

'What are you laughing at?'

'Well, you get the biggest selection, that way. Everyone who ever wrote a symphony must have written a first, but some of them didn't get past three or four. If you collected ninth symphonies, say, you wouldn't have so many to choose from.'

'I don't choose. I buy all the first symphonies.'

'Even if you don't like them?'

'In a lifetime,' Mrs Tulkinghorne said, 'I have heard them all. I have even heard the complete symphonies of Haydn and Mozart, but the Classicists don't count. I always come back to the first symphonies – which is more than the composers could.'

'What do you mean?' Mrs Tulkinghorne had returned to her divan and was sitting urgently on the edge, the coffee mug gripped in clenched hands. He wished more than ever that he could push his chair back. 'Surely it *was* the classical composers – people like Haydn and Mozart – who probably never heard their work played more than once ... who couldn't go back. Throwaway music.' He sometimes found that thought unbearable. No tapes for Haydn, no discs, no sheet music sales, even. Every one of his glorious hundred and four played once and forgotten instantly by the tin-eared nobs who commissioned them.

'No, I don't mean that,' Mrs Tulkinghorne said. 'The classical composers are without passion. But the others, Bruckner, Schubert, Beethoven, Sibelius, Mahler ... it all went into their first symphonies and they never got it back again.'

'What did? What was it?'

'If you don't know I can't tell you. But you wouldn't

have noticed it, would you? Your First Symphony is still to come, I suppose.'

'*My* First Symphony?' He must have lost her thread, somewhere. 'I'm doing languages. I love music, of course, but I –'

'I am not talking about music,' Mrs Tulkinghorne interrupted. 'Whatever you do in your life, the first time you do it – however badly – will be your First Symphony. There must be so many things you haven't done even once, yet, whatever you tell your friends, and that first time, you'll never recapture it, never, though you'll try all your life. Have some more coffee.' '

'I ought to get back,' he said.

'Have some more coffee.' She was into the galley and there again before he could stop her, with her coffee pot and his milk jug. 'It's so nice to have someone to talk to. John – my husband – isn't very interested in music. He's an amateur botanist – though I suppose you'd have to be an amateur in the true sense of the word to be a botanist at all. Plants don't lead very exciting lives, do they, and if they're not dull they're vile. Great hot sweating things, like flesh.'

Her shaking hand poured coffee into his mug and down his leg. He could not move; the chair paralysed him, but a manic instinct for self-preservation stopped his scream in his throat. If she noticed what she had done she would mop him up, her hand on his thigh.

'That's probably what happened to him, my husband. He's got sidetracked by a rare plant.'

'I don't think we have any rare plants round here.'

'Oh, you must have. I've noticed dozens this week that we never see at home.'

He smiled tremulously. 'That doesn't mean they're rare.'

Prokofiev was getting into his stride. 'Listen,' Mrs Tulkinghorne cried. 'Doesn't this prove everything I've said?'

'It is called the "Classical",' he reminded her, maliciously. 'Prokofiev thought he was writing in the style of Haydn.'

'It's like nothing else he ever wrote.'

'I don't know. "Three Oranges" is very lively . . . the "Cinderella" suites . . .'

'It's not just liveliness. It's the first time; you can tell it's his first time, like the Mahler. It's all before him, everything seems possible. Did you know –' she asked, suddenly, interrupting herself, '– Mahler was afraid to write a ninth symphony?'

'Afraid?'

'Afraid it would be his last. Beethoven died after his Ninth, and Bruckner. When it was time for Mahler's Ninth he wrote *Das Lied von der Erde* instead. Do you know it?'

He knew it. 'Yes. *The Song of the Earth*.'

'He shouldn't have done that,' said Mrs Tulkinghorne. 'It didn't do him any good. He had to write a ninth symphony in the end and it wasn't his best. His Tenth was never even finished . . .' She was on her knees now, in the middle of a little hand-woven rug, as if praying to him.

Her body was girlish in the white sun dress, but the low neckline exposed a sad landscape of indelible freckles and thread veins. A look of alarm crossed her face, ageing it as it took her unawares.

'What time is it?'

'I don't know. I left my watch at home. It must be getting on for nine.'

'I didn't realize how late it was.'

He thought of school and erased it. 'Nine o'clock is pretty early.'

'Not for breakfast. This –' she indicated the coffee pot '– is my breakfast. One doesn't normally entertain strangers to breakfast.'

'I'm a neighbour really.' He tried to pacify her. 'Temporarily, at any rate.'

'I don't know what John, my husband, would think. He ought to be back soon. Perhaps you'd better go.'

'He won't mind, will he?'

'I don't know what he'd *think*. Have you finished your coffee?'

She stood up and gazed anxiously out of the cabin window, across the meadow, towards the house. He was being thrown out, his coffee not even begun. Trying to recover the initiative, he said, 'Well, perhaps I ought to be moving. I'll be late for school.'

'You're still at school? I thought you were older,' she said vaguely. 'So *all* your first times are still to come? Yes, you *had* better go . . . I'd no idea . . .'

They went into the galley. In unseasonable haste now she poured the remainder of the milk into an empty bottle, rinsed out the jug and put the eggs into an empty polystyrene carton that she took from a cupboard by the sink.

'Really, it wouldn't do if you ran into him, would it?' He began to envisage an incensed gorilla among the buttercups, as he was ushered up the three steps, into the cockpit and from there to the deck, to the bank. As if they were a parting gift she reached up and thrust into his hands the bowl and the jug.

'Hurry back. Your mother will wonder what you've been doing.'

'She won't,' he assured her. 'She won't even notice how long I've been gone. She probably thinks I've come back and gone on to school.'

'I'm sure she wouldn't approve of my keeping you down here, alone with me. Goodbye . . . Nicholas.'

'Goodbye, Mrs Tulkinghorne.' The boat rocked slightly, and she was gone. Abruptly, the Prokofiev stopped in mid-movement.

As he turned to cross the meadow he saw, coming the other way, a man stepping briskly through the buttercups and lady's smocks. Anxious to put as great a distance as possible between himself and Mrs Tulkinghorne, Nicholas began to walk rapidly along the path realizing, only when he saw the fuel can at his side, that this must be Mr Tulkinghorne, returning from his search for diesel. He slackened his pace. Mr Tulkinghorne strode on, whistling, through the shining meadow, the sun in his eyes. He was only a yard or two from Nicholas when he caught sight of him.

'Good morning,' Mr Tulkinghorne said.

'Good morning,' Nicholas said.

'Been down to the boat?' said Mr Tulkinghorne.

'You must be Mr Tulkinghorne,' said Nicholas.

'That's right.' Mr Tulkinghorne did not look very old; younger than his wife, possibly. He threw back his shoulders. Nicholas thought again of proprietorial male gorillas and waited for Mr Tulkinghorne to put down his fuel can and beat his chest. Almost he heard the virile rhythm boom across the broad.

'Went for diesel,' said the gorilla, a lean man, after all, with little hair on him. 'Got lost coming back. Asked the way up at your place. Y'mother said I might run into you.'

'I was only delivering milk and eggs,' Nicholas said, waving his crockery defensively.

'Very good of you. Hope the silly woman remembered to pay.'

'Your wife? Yes, of course.' He remembered suddenly that she had not.

'Sister,' Mr Tulkinghorne said. He looked down at the flowers round his knees. 'What's the local name for these?'

'Lady's smocks.' Nicholas thought of his mother, like an overcrowded bell tent in her own lady's smock. Widowed ten years, she still looked married.

'We call 'em milkmaids back home,' Mr Tulkinghorne said. '*Cardamine pratensis.* Good morning to you.' They parted on the path across the meadow like figures in a drawing repositioned by an artist who found them uncongenial so close together.

Nicholas surprised his mother in the kitchen, guiltily pouring a glass of chilled Piesporter.

'At this hour?' he asked, reprovingly, and looked at the clock. It was just after nine.

'It's so hot,' she excused herself. 'I wondered when you'd show up. What on earth have you been doing?'

'I stopped for coffee.'

'I thought she must be seducing you.'

Nicholas frowned as he put the jug and bowl in the sink. 'We were listening to records. Mahler's First, Prokofiev's First –'

'All firsts?'

'As a matter of fact, yes. Mrs Tulkinghorne's got a thing about first symphonies, that composers get something into their first symphonies that they never have again. She said it was the same with everything we do for the first time.'

'Mrs Tulkinghorne? What a mouthful.'

'And that there's something final about your ninth.'

'Mrs T.'s written her Ninth Symphony, poor love,' his mother said, turning towards the door. 'She's on to fantasias now.'

He wondered how much she had guessed. 'Aren't you writing fantasias?'

His mother, the novelist, smiled in the doorway. 'I write lies,' she said, 'and get paid for it. Not quite the same thing. Aren't you going to school?'

'I'll have a headache.'

'Make it a good one. There's another glass of this left in the bottle.'

Nicholas sat on in the empty kitchen with the bottle before him on the scrubbed table. His mother was wrong. Mrs Tulkinghorne, or Miss Tulkinghorne as he supposed she must be, had not written her Ninth Symphony, or even her First. He raised his glass to the open window and heard, distantly, the pulse of a diesel engine moving away across the water.

[7]

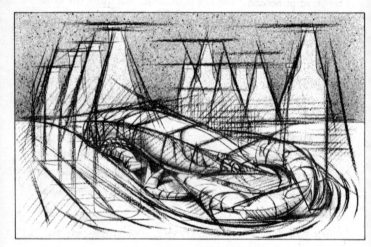

Still Life:
Remote Control

At the lower end of the High Street the Art College stood
between the Gas Board showrooms and the Maid of Kent.
The frontage, an absent-minded Neo-Gothic doodle, was
slightly tilted in common with its neighbours which gave a
fair indication of conditions inside and suggested, with
some probability, that the district was gradually subsiding
into the river.

Ainsley and Cadman stepped out of the saloon bar of the Maid of Kent.

'Hang on,' said Cadman, turning a full circle on the spot, and scurried inside again. Ainsley waited on the pavement and watched the students scrambling out of the doorway that led to the public bar. Cadman reappeared with a length of blue linen slung over his shoulder.

'Your toga?' said Ainsley, falling into step beside him.

'What? No, I need it for class this afternoon,' said Cadman. He became self-conscious of the drape and tucked it under his arm.

'Life class?' Ainsley knew that Cadman liked to pose his models with pieces of fabric hanging about their persons; he had himself loaned a pair of chenille curtains for that purpose.

'Still life, first years,' said Cadman, as they entered the college by the front door. The students had to go round to the back where the three caretakers, Ted, George and Cyril, looked out from their basement room like Cerberus at the gate of Hades. 'They're very enthusiastic about bringing their own subjects but they always forget about the drapes. They've got no idea of texture.'

'Shocking,' said Ainsley, who had no idea of texture either. He taught Liberal Studies in a rickety crow's nest at the top of the building.

'No idea of anything really,' Cadman went on. 'All chat and never a thought between them. Look at Carlow.'

'Dick Carlow? I rather like Carlow,' said Ainsley. 'I should have said he was full of ideas.'

'I dare say, but no ideas about painting. He knows he can draw and he thinks that's enough, thank you very much. All his paintings look like drawings; I want to bang my head on the wall after a session with him,' said Cadman. His eyes drew into feverish slits at the thought of it.

'Naughty Dick,' said Ainsley.

'I'm having a blitz on him this afternoon,' Cadman confided. 'All out war, him or me. I'll have him painting whether he likes it or not. I shall tell him: "This is an art school! not a drawing office."'

'You do that,' said Ainsley. At that moment the student Carlow came out of a side turning that led to the Liberal Studies department.

'What have you been up to in there?' said Cadman.

'Just having a little think, Mr Cadman,' said Carlow, loping ahead with his knees slightly bent in the manner of a man raised among pickpockets. Ainsley turned aside, towards the staircase, and Cadman followed Carlow round the corner and into the studio where the first-year class was assembling. Twenty downy faces turned towards him in amiable greeting, but Cadman's eye was drawn to the dark den behind the model's throne where Carlow had gone to earth. Carlow sat down industriously but several of his friends were still loafing about: Roland Hereson, the college corn-treader, in his armour-plated boots that turned up at the toes, Hugh Furnival with his frightful old-maid's smile, Charles Keller, Cheerful Charlie Keller, Buddy Holly glasses see-sawing on the brink of his nose.

'Come out of that, you lazy beasts,' said Cadman. 'You should be in your places and ready to start by one-thirty.' They edged past him. Hereson was carrying a dead dog-fish by the tail.

'What's that for?'

'Still life, Mr Cadman,' said Hereson. 'You asked us to bring our own subjects. I got it from my friend with the fishing boat.' He cleared a path to his easel by means of well-placed jabs with the dog-fish. Keller followed him with a melon in his hands.

'Are you going to paint that or eat it?'

'Both, Mr Cadman,' said Keller with a lichenous grin. 'Roland's friend got it for us.'

Hereson's wants were supplied by a circle of unseen friends. My friend with the boat, my friend the gunsmith, my friend the public analyst . . . Cadman imagined them herded together in medieval proximity under a low-beamed ceiling, where a cauldron steamed over an open fire and friends sidled to and fro with contraband consignments of guns, fish, gin, cement . . . my friend the brick-layer, my friend the Chief Constable.

Keller, who had also been to the Maid of Kent, passed by on a blast of fiery breath followed by Hugh Furnival, tiny Hugh, who haunted cemeteries with his sketch book and came to class with pictures of funerals and open graves.

Cadman believed that it was his life's ambition to witness an exhumation.

Only Carlow was left in the corner, an immaculate squirrel in elastic-sided boots, manipulating the extreme end of a long paintbrush. Other students were flecked and freckled to the elbow, to the shoulder. No paint ever soiled Carlow's fastidious fingers.

'And what are you doing?' said Cadman. Carlow glanced up and met his look with a translucent eye.

'I'm painting a little picture, Mr Cadman,' he said.

'And why are you using oils?' First-year students were supposed to paint in gouache, for their own protection perhaps, in case the turpentine fumes went to their heads and led them to believe that they were artists.

'I don't know, Mr Cadman,' said Carlow, lifting his eyebrows and gazing in surprise at his palette as though by transubstantiation the water colour had turned to oil. He had assembled his own still life, a livid lobster disposed among a group of clear glass bottles.

'That lobster's still alive,' said Cadman, extending his neck in order to see Carlow's painting, which he was cleverly concealing beneath the palette.

'Oh no, I don't think so, Mr Cadman,' said Carlow. 'Roland's friend told me it was dead.' He reversed his paintbrush and tapped authoritatively on the shell with the butt. 'Anyone in there? Come out please. This gentleman wants to speak to you. No, it's definitely dead.' He spread his hands regretfully.

'Why isn't it red then?' said Cadman, with a vision of the creature leaving the premises during the afternoon. 'Lobsters have to be boiled.'

'I imagine it died of natural causes,' said Carlow. 'He'd have flogged it, otherwise.'

'How can you see anything in that hole?' The studio was lit by sloping skylights that faced north. To the disadvantages offered by a cloudy sky, Carlow had added the generous shadow of a plaster Venus de Milo. 'Come further out where you'll get a good light.'

'No thank you,' said Carlow, the imperturbable craftsman, demure and courteous. 'I started this before lunch. I don't want to change it now.'

'Well, if you must lurk . . .' said Cadman. 'Don't get too involved with it, though. You may find you've been a little over-hasty.' He backed out of the corner, high-stepping over stools. The class noticed him coming and stopped talking, settling into their places around the room, with the exception of Hereson and Keller who began to wrangle over the dog-fish, tugging at it savagely from either end.

'Now stop that. Stop it,' cried Cadman. His voice cracked disloyally. 'Put that thing down, Roland. Charlie. Charles!' Keller, still susceptible to a schoolmasterly tone, let go of the tail. Hereson sat down with the fish in his arms, its head resting against his shoulder like a newly fed baby.

'Now, yes. I want a new approach today,' said Cadman. 'You've been coming in here every Wednesday for the last five months; you sit down at your easels and you paint pictures. I don't want to see any pictures today.' He looked across the class to where Carlow sat in the shadows. 'No pictures,' he repeated. 'Take instead a dozen sheets of newsprint and let's see you make some impressions. Approach your subjects from every angle – turn them upside down. Don't try to finish anything, I want you to discard as much as you keep. I don't care,' he went on recklessly, 'if you discard everything. This is a day for experiments. You are becoming arid, stereotyped. I can always recognize your work before I see the name on it. Confuse me.'

'A pleasure, my dear sir, a pleasure,' murmured Furnival, knotted up with midnight villainy. He leaned across to Hereson. 'You know, Leonardo didn't really paint the Mona Lisa. It was Botticelli, working in the style of Brueghel the Elder, to confuse the pope.'

'Ow, shut up,' said Cadman. 'You know perfectly well what I mean. I've been trying to loosen you up for weeks. Today I'm putting my foot down. No pictures. Draw with your left hands for a change, hold the brushes in your toes – put your shoe on, Keller. Now, Miss Gilbert, Miss Lewington, and you Furnival, take a walk round your subjects. You may find you get a more interesting view from the back.'

Miss Gilbert had set up a fox fur wound cosily round a roadmender's lamp, with cedar cones scattered about.

'Exhilarating contrast of textures, there,' said Cadman.

'Try to work from an angle that disguises the identity of the objects. Concentrate on those textures.'

Miss Gilbert nodded submissively. Experimenting with dress reform she was wearing a tube of green velvet, stapled together at the seams.

'Is that quite comfortable?' he asked.

'No,' said Miss Gilbert. She carried the fox fur away and petted it affectionately as she prowled about the room.

Cadman arranged his blue drape over the throne and invited the class to arrange their groups upon it. 'Let's see you all treat it differently,' he suggested. 'No, Roland, not that,' he said, as he saw Hereson sneaking up with the dog-fish. 'Put it on some newspaper.' He left them to it and climbed over the stools to reach Carlow. The lobster was where he had last seen it, squatting among the bottles, and Carlow was in the same position, painting the same picture.

'Didn't you hear what I was just saying?' demanded Cadman. Carlow's eyes flickered.

'Yes, Mr Cadman.'

'But you haven't done anything about it.'

'Yes I have.' Carlow lifted his board and turned it for Cadman's inspection. The work in progress was a masterly exhibition of misplaced self-confidence. Carlow was a draughtsman and he painted in the style of a draughtsman, every elegant stroke of the brush falling exactly where he intended. Faultless, unfaultable, and well aware of it.

'That isn't what I want at all,' said Cadman.

'It's what I want, Mr Cadman,' said Carlow, the statement of his dislike as formal and precise as his painting.

Cadman ground his fingers together.

'Leave it. I don't want you to go on. Get some paper and start again from a different aspect.' His enthusiasm overcame his anger. 'Get up above it. Stand on the table and look down on it. Turn some of the bottles on their sides – look, scatter them – and move that lobster . . .'

His hand stretched out to illustrate his meaning and Carlow's flat fingers came down across his wrist.

'I'll do it.'

'Go on then.' Under Cadman's gaze, Carlow laid aside his board and broke up the group. Satisfied, Cadman left him to sulk.

As soon as Cadman's back was turned, Carlow got up, replaced the bottles and tenderly straightened the lobster's claws; easily done since he had had the foresight to draw round them with a piece of chalk before he started work. Then he went on with his painting. While the others wielded hog-hair brushes with all the finesse of bricklayers spreading mortar, he worked with a number three sable, his name, Richard Carlow, minutely incised on the handle.

Cadman bounded across the room to Miss Lewington, call me Lulu, who was crawling about on a carpet of newsprint pushing a tray of ink bottles before her.

'Mind where you put your feet,' said Miss Lewington who understood that since she was being experimental she might be offensive as well. Only the dullards had to be polite. Cadman stooped and stammered.

'Oh, that's good. That's intelligent. What are you using, rulers dipped in ink? Very definitive . . .' Charlie paddled after him, droning in his ear.

'Sir, sir, 'ere sir . . .'

'Just a minute, Keller. Now, Lulu, be a bit daring and bring in a new texture. Got any charcoal? Right, now hold it lengthways and sweep . . . What are you up to, Hereson?'

'Powdered graphite,' said Hereson. 'I rub it into the paper and then draw with the putty rubber.'

With one leap, Cadman was by his side.

'Oh, that's exciting, that's good . . .'

''Ere, sir, 'ere,' intoned Charlie, mournful in limbo. ''Ere, you was saying?'

'What?' Cadman hurtled away again.

'Look at this, Lulu,' said Hereson. He moulded his putty rubber into various repellent shapes and shunted them up and down the drawing board.

'I think you're foul,' said Miss Lewington, fiercely pink and turning away.

'Thought you'd recognize it,' said Hereson pleasantly. He hummed a little tune under his breath.

Carlow, in command and self-sufficient behind his easel, divided his attention between Cadman and the lobster. The lobster, distorted though it seemed behind the bottles, was giving him no trouble, but Cadman, with the aimless skips of a spring lambkin, was working his way back towards the corner. A brief gambol with Miss Gilbert who was laying on colour with the tail of the fox fur – 'It's a brush, isn't it? That's a joke,' she explained patiently – and the anxious, beardless face was once more hovering over his shoulder.

'Oh,' said Cadman. He stared at Carlow's little hymn to perfection. 'I thought I made myself perfectly clear.'

'Yes, Mr Cadman.'

'I don't want any pictures today.'

'This is for my half-yearly assessment,' said Carlow, lowering a portcullis of sharp eyelashes.

'I'm not interested in your half-yearly assessment. This picture is exactly the same as all the other pictures that you do in my class, in the life class, in the pictorial composition class. You won't experiment. You're sterilizing yourself.' He insinuated his head between Carlow and the painting. For all the reaction he got, there might have been a dead man behind the portcullis. 'Don't think I'm criticizing you.'

'No, Mr Cadman. I don't think that.'

'No one's quarrelling with your technique. You must stretch yourself, expand. You work with your hands – what are you doing with your head?' Cadman folded himself into a quivering question mark and crouched down, wheedlingly. 'Take Keller, for instance. He hasn't an ounce of your talent, but every mark he makes on the paper is a new experience for him. He's treading in new territory.'

Keller was, in fact, treading on a tube of titanium white. Carlow wondered which end would give way first and tucked up his feet under him.

'But you,' said Cadman, incensed by his inattention, 'you haven't made a single discovery since you first set foot in the building. You're as arrogant as an old master. I can tell you right now what your assessment will be: no progress. No progress!'

'I see.' Carlow set one hand upon the other in his lap, a silent gesture of uninterest. In a rage, Cadman looked round for a weapon and saw on the radiator an ill-used hog-hair brush congealing in a jam jar. Seizing it by the hilt he stabbed it into the heart of Carlow's silken oils and began to jab, thrust, stir, slash, score.

'There. There. There. Knock your colours in, bang them down, bash them on. Bring it alive. Take it by the throat and shake it alive!'

Carlow said nothing. Out of Cadman's view his hands were locked together under the drawing board.

'Attack it. Be brutal. Stand up and run at it, head down.' Cadman reeled and gasped, knocking hair out of his eyes. Carlow stood up as requested, his forefingers lined up guardsmanly with his trousers seams.

'Now look at it. Look at it.' Cadman stood back, certain that there were no means by which Carlow could reassemble his original design. 'The whole thing's moving now; surging. Feel the power behind the mass . . . the thrust . . . the urge.' He made soaring spires with his arms, battened his fingers into an arcade and stared madly down it, shook hooked hands under Carlow's nose.

'It's only a lobster, Mr Cadman,' said Carlow. His painting, constructed with the precision of an architect's drawing, had been reduced to a bomb site, blasted, a heap of rubble.

'No, it's not. Don't think of it as a lobster.'

'Very difficult to think of it as anything at all now,' said Carlow.

'And stop footling with that whisker.' Cadman flicked irritably at the number three sable. 'I'd rather see you using a decorator's brush.'

He turned back to the rest of the class who were watching him happily. For all those who admired Carlow and envied his innate skill, there were as many who regarded him as a hack and despised the innate skill which they were acquiring so painfully.

'Come on, come on, get down to it you idle lot,' said Cadman. 'This is nothing to do with you.' He looked at the clock above the door. 'Ow, it's nearly two forty-five. Take your break now.'

The studio emptied rapidly as the class went to take its break in the Arcadia Coffee Bar, on the far side of the Gas Board showrooms. It was closer than the college canteen which moved further away every year as the building expanded, and now occupied a remote pre-fab at the end of the car park.

Carlow remained in the corner, knuckles set against his

teeth and his mouth drawn down in a furious smile. At last he permitted himself to take a little exercise, and walked thoughtfully about the studio. He had originally taken possession of the corner to be out of Cadman's way, but having retreated into his citadel he was now besieged. Every member of the class with his dozen sheets of newsprint had claimed every square foot of the floor. Carlow walked in anger, treading with care round the edges of the newsprint, longing to stamp on it.

Thanks to his own low cunning he had the worst position in the room, while those who needed it least had the best of the light. Rain was dribbling down the glass slope of the skylights and his own corner had become a dismal canyon. Charlie, on the other hand, had a perfect view of the depressing things that he was doing.

Chin on fist, Carlow regarded Charlie's efforts. Charlie was clearly becoming bored. Given the additional fact that Charlie couldn't draw anyway, he must be having a miserable afternoon. Nearby were Roland's impressions of the dog-fish. He had given up graphite for the livelier medium of poster paint, but in spite of this the fish looked progressively more dead in each sketch, a world-weary demi-mondain that had committed suicide out of sheer ennui.

Carlow moved on. Hugh Furnival played the clarinet in his spare time and played it well. Today he was drawing it, badly. Carlow nodded at the clarinet and went back to his corner where he took out a freshly primed board and set it up on his easel. When the class returned, Cadman swaying among them, he was hard at work and scarcely looked up.

Cadman was in demand. Shaking the rain from his hair like a lean wet hound he rushed about the studio responding to eager requests: advise, advise; meaning, admire, admire. Cadman, perversely, kept squinting towards the corner where Carlow sat with his head well down, wanting none of it.

Charlie dogged him with a sheaf of dusty newsprint but Cadman, attracted like a bent pin to a magnet, was heading for Carlow. He weaseled round the Venus de Milo, beady-eyed.

'Oh, that's better, that's good, that's intelligent. Yes, yes, yes.'

'I'm glad you like it,' said Carlow with a modest inclination of the head.

'Scumbles,' said Cadman. 'What are you using? Oil again . . . ?' His attention was diverted by Furnival, hovering. 'Just a minute . . . I'll be back . . . Carry on . . . Lovely texture.' He could afford to be gracious.

Roland filtered through a crack between wall and easel. He looked at Carlow's work with his head on one side.

'Ow, that's nice. Ow, that's clever. Ow!' As a mimic, Roland was more vindictive than accurate but his victims could always identify themselves. He resumed his own voice. 'What a mess.'

'I might say the same about your fish,' said Carlow.

'Do you know what he said about it?' Roland jerked his thumb at Cadman. 'He said it was moribund.'

'So it is. Nothing looks deader than a dead fish. It's the eyes that do it,' said Carlow.

'I can't paint eyes.'

'So I noticed. You ought to put a real one in.'

'What, on the painting? One of Cadman's, I suppose.' Roland looked reflective and made eye-gouging gestures. Carlow raised his bottle of turpentine and let a few drops fall on the board.

'What are you doing?' said Roland, plaintively.

'Scumbles,' said Carlow, rubbing at the paint with the corner of a paint rag.

'Is that what he said?'

'That's what I think he said. If I could persuade him down the scale a little I might be certain.' Cadman's conversation was carried on in the querulous squeal of a hunting bat. 'Half of what he says is out of our range.'

'I bet little dogs come running when he speaks,' said Roland. 'Oh look, Gilbert's got him.'

Carlow looked round the easel. Miss Gilbert, grown skittish, was flirting her fox-tail at the tutor and Cadman, ever a prey to large young women, stood wavering with one leg wound round the other in cruel embarrassment, apparently trying to screw himself into the floor.

'You wouldn't think he could balance so well on those little feet,' said Carlow.

'He's swaying a bit.'

'I wonder where his centre of gravity is?'

'Shall we find out?'

'Just wing him and see which way he falls.' Roland oozed out of the aperture and started across the room, knees akimbo. Next moment Cadman was spinning out of control; one outflung arm struck an easel and dislodged the rampart of poster paint pots that Roland had erected to ward off boredom.

'Oh my God. Oh, what a mess. I'm sorry, Hereson.'

Roland, who had been mixing dust from the floor with his pigment to produce a gritty impasto, dabbed a tentative finger in the sludge from the overturned pots.

'It's all right, Mr Cadman. I think you've improved it, if anything.'

Charlie ran to help clear up, rallying round trouble in true Charlie fashion. He cut a wide swathe through the class with a long-handled mop and Carlow silently urged him on. Furnival ducked into the corner to be out of Charlie's way.

'Hullo, Hugh. What are you looking so fed up about?'

'That man's a fidget,' said Hugh, scowling at Cadman who was still gyrating in the middle of the floor.

'Doesn't he like your pretty pictures, then?'

'He doesn't like the same thing five minutes running,' said Hugh.

'He doesn't like you at all,' Carlow pointed out. 'Hours at a time.'

'It's that damn clarinet,' said Hugh. 'I've drawn it three

different times from three different angles; ink, charcoal, conté crayon. It always looks the same. There's not a lot you can do with a clarinet.'

'There's not a lot you can do with a lobster.'

'Eat it?'

'This one died of natural causes,' said Carlow. 'Why don't you give us a tune?'

'Uh?'

'Give us a tune. On your hooter.' He knew the idea would need time to take root.

'I want to get on with my pictorial comp. for the assessment. It's meant to be handed in tomorrow morning,' said Hugh. His work was never finished on time. 'What do you think will happen if I don't?'

'Trouble,' said Carlow, scrubbing at his work with the paint rag. 'Why don't you do it now? There's three quarters of an hour to go and you could always stay after four o'clock.'

'He won't like that.' Hugh glanced over his shoulder to where Cadman strutted and pecked like a long-legged wading bird, dipping for fish.

'He won't notice. Tell him you're experimenting with a new technique.'

'But it's a picture of the cathedral,' said Hugh.

'You tell him it's a clarinet and he'll believe you. An Early English clarinet with Norman columns and Perpendicular windows.'

'Come on, come on, work, work, work,' sang Cadman.

'Miss Lewington, someone has stood in your burnt sienna.'

Hugh went back to his place and Carlow saw him take a half finished painting from his folder and set it on his easel in place of the three clarinets: ink, charcoal, conté crayon.

'And how are you getting on?' said Cadman, in his ear. Carlow jumped.

'Nicely, thank you.' He refused to look round.

'May I see it?' Cadman's face slanted sideways in anticipation.

'Of course.' He handed over the board, still watching Furnival's extraordinarily obvious efforts to appear unobtrusive.

'Lovely, lovely. That colour sings.' His fingers ran up and down imaginary ladders. 'You do realize, don't you, that nothing you've done up till now even approaches this for vigour?' A terrific swipe with the right fist, inches from Carlow's right ear. 'You need to stand away from it. Look, I'll take it to the other side of the room and you have a good stare.' He whisked the board away and pranced off to stand in the far corner with the board held high above his head. 'Just a moment, you people. I want you to take a look at this.' Every head turned towards him and a cloud of little hisses and gasps rose from among them and seemed to hang in the air.

'Siiiiings,' cried Cadman, on a high note. 'Come on, admit it, Richard. You've never done anything like this before, now have you?'

'I certainly haven't, Mr Cadman,' said Carlow. Out of

the corner of his eye he could just see the remains of his earlier work trickling forlornly over the feet of Venus.

'He hates admitting it,' said Cadman, gleefully. 'Can't tell him anything.' He frisked back to Carlow on lightsome toes and stood the painting against the wall.

'Can't I have it back?' Carlow reached out to take it up.

'No. Do another one.'

'But I haven't finished that, yet.'

'Don't touch it,' said Cadman. 'I know you,' he said, craftily. 'You'll worry it to death. You'll work and work at it until it looks just like all the others. I'm not going to give up now I've got you started.' He picked up the painting and teasingly moved it a few inches to the right. 'Don't lay a finger on it.'

He caught sight of Miss Gilbert's fox painting.

'That's exciting, that's interesting.'

Keller put his head round the easel. 'What's so special about you, then? Every time I show him something he says "Ow, that's interesting" and slopes off.'

'I should be so lucky,' said Carlow. 'You ought to do him some textures. He likes textures. What are you painting?'

'It was the melon, but Roland's eaten half of it. Now I'm stuck with that rotten fish.'

'It's a very nice fish.'

'Not any more,' said Charlie. 'We've had it three days and it's going off. Roland won't go near it.'

'I'll tell you what you ought to do,' said Carlow. 'Put the paint on the fish. Then take a print off it.'

'You're joking.'

'No I'm not. You'll get textures like you never saw before.' Charlie looked doubtful. 'Go on, he'll love it.'

Cadman came up on Hugh from behind. 'And what's this?'

'I thought I'd take a few moments off from my clarinet,' said Hugh, uneasily.

'Isn't that your pictorial comp.? Who said you could work on it in my still life class?'

Since Carlow had told him, Hugh was unable to reply. He spread a shifty arm across the painting and regarded the ceiling.

'Well, you'd better let me see it,' said Cadman, peevishly, enticed in spite of himself by what little he could make out between Hugh's fingers. 'I suppose you've got to hand it in tomorrow?'

'I didn't want to waste time,' said Hugh.

'Waste time? My God, if you weren't so path-o-log-i-call-y lazy you'd have been finished days ago. Whose time are you wasting now, may I ask?'

'I didn't seem to be making much headway with the clarinet.'

'You don't seem to make much headway with anything,' said Cadman, pushing the arm to one side. His expression changed. 'I don't know, though. This is very unusual, very different.'

'It's a cathedral,' said Hugh quickly, before Cadman could alter his opinion. 'This nice bit of chiaroscuro is the effect of the stained-glass windows on the bishop's throne. That umbrageous blot represents the shadowed aisles, and this murky old gentleman is a verger.'

Cadman laid his hands on the painting as if absorbing its virtue, and went cross-eyed with excitement.

'I ought to be very cross with you, Furnival, but it is exciting. The whole thing seems to be moving. I don't know about the verger; he's a little obvious, but the rest is impressionistic, very impressionistic. If you toned the red down there . . . and brought up the blues to balance the background . . . the effect of that verger though . . . very clotted. Can you scrape him down?'

'I'm rather fond of that verger,' said Hugh. 'Still, yes, I could scrape him down.'

'He is a bit clotted. Use a razor blade – what are you doing, Keller?'

'Textures, Mr Cadman,' said Charlie, laying a worm of cobalt blue down the middle of the dog-fish.

Alerted by the mention of textures Cadman ran to see what was happening.

'Do you think that cobalt is a good idea, Keller?'

Hugh went to borrow a blade from Carlow. He propped himself against the Venus de Milo and chipped away glumly.

'If I go on like this the whole verger will come off in a lump.'

'Put it under the tap,' said Carlow. 'That way you can soften him up and paint over him when he dries off.'

Hugh went to the sink by the door and collided with Hereson who was on his way out of the room.

'Hey, where are you off to, Hereson?' said Cadman, knowing that Roland was liable to abandon the class if he felt he had outdistanced his genius before the end of the session.

'Just popping out to the lavatory,' said Roland, with a reassuring wave of the hand.

''Ere sir, what did you say?' demanded Charlie, left in the lurch again.

'That cobalt. Won't it be a bit obvious?'

'Won't it just?' muttered Carlow.

Cadman ran his finger along the dog-fish.

'Where's its eye gone?'

'Some so-and-so must have nicked it,' said Charlie, ready to dismantle the room in order to find it, but Cadman had moved on again.

'Sir!'

Hugh prepared to soften up his verger. The sink was a wide, shallow basin with a silted-up wastepipe that overflowed more readily than tears. It was fed by a single tap that seemed to be connected to a pipe in the cloakroom for when anyone flushed a lavatory the flow into the sink was reduced to a trickle. By means of judiciously scheduled chain-pulling, a malicious student could keep the studio in a state of indefinite drought.

Hugh held his picture, still pinned to its board, under the thin spindle of water. On the other side of the wall a cistern could be heard stertorously replenishing itself. He let the water play over the verger who, raised in high relief by the accretions of black and prussian blue, began to disintegrate. As he was about to turn off the tap the cistern was suddenly filled, the water gushed out and the verger exploded in an oily blue-black geyser that spattered the walls.

Hugh wrestled with the tap to rescue the remains of his cathedral.

'Oh God.' Cadman was wiping paint out of his eyes. 'How bloody stupid can you get, Furnival?'

'It's ruined,' said Hugh, bitterly contemplating the squid-like emissions of his verger.

'I said scrape it, not drown it.'

The air was split by a loud flat smack. Charlie, in pursuit of texture, had grown tired of dabbing at the dog-fish. He picked it up by the tail, whirled it round his head and brought it down across his drawing board.

'Textures you want – textures you get,' said Carlow to no one in particular.

Cadman stepped aside from Charlie's second swing and found himself face to face with Roland's latest painting of the dog-fish, enlivened by a single sardonic eye that Roland had prised from the model and embedded in the paint.

Charlie administered more cobalt and swung his fish again. A wide space opened all round him as the rest of the class dived out of range in an attempt to save their own work. A water pot spun across the floor and landed at

Cadman's feet so accurately that it might have been thrown. Miss Lewington stepped into the succulent hemisphere of Roland's half-eaten melon.

At the third blow the fish burst, covering everything inside a three-yard radius with truly astonishing textures.

Miss Gilbert, dappled with fish and verger, began to scream and Cadman, only a semitone lower, screamed too.

'Get out of it. All of you. Clear up. I never saw anything . . .'

Hugh cupped his hand to his ear, dropped his painting and picked up the clarinet.

'Can you hold that note a moment, Mr Cadman?' A plaintive honking filled the air, and echoed round the studio.

Carlow picked his way through the debris, flicking fish from his sleeve.

'Excuse me, Mr Cadman?'

'What do you want?' said Cadman.

'Would you mind if I stayed a little late, after four o'clock? I'd like to finish my assessment work, if it wouldn't cause too much trouble. I won't make a mess.' His bland blue eyes seemed to ignore, with enormous tact, the wreckage of the still life class.

'Oh, do what you like,' said Cadman, banging his hands against his ears. Roland had returned, cheeping like a little bird, and he was trying to locate the insane tweeting.

'And may I use my number three sable?'

'I said do what you like. I can't be bothered with any of you – Keller, get that disgusting thing out of here.' He turned away. 'Do what you like.'

'Thank you, Mr Cadman,' said Carlow, seating himself at his easel. The rainstorm had passed and the late sun cast a serene reflection over the Venus de Milo. 'I usually do,' he added. 'In the end.'

[8]

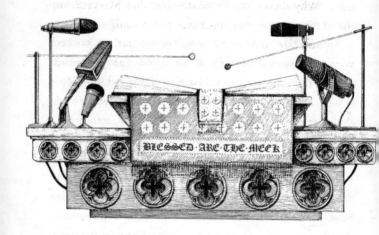

A Little Misunderstanding

'God won't bless them for working on a Sunday,' Miss Veal remarked, as the car passed a little shop where two men on stepladders were painting the fascia. She made her observation in a curiously unemphatic voice, without outrage or even disapproval, merely stating an unarguable fact, much as she might have commented upon the fine evening weather. Kipper wondered why she had bothered to speak; saying it had done nothing to change the situation. Why didn't Miss Veal demand that Mr Jack stop the car on the instant, leap out and harangue the two insouciant labourers on the subject of damnation? Mr Jack very sensibly said nothing at all as the car proceeded, leaving the men to their Sabbath-breaking, while Kipper turned and watched them through the rear window. At the other end of the seat Cobbold posed, aloof, fastidious, a sardonic aristocrat conveyed in a tumbril to the guillotine, while the she-wolves knitted at his feet.

This withdrawal from glum reality was one of Cobbold's *tableaux vivants* (less impressive than his crazed Ayatollah but also less improbable, since it demanded nothing more than icy paralysis) which he was maintaining for the benefit of Mr Jack, eyeball to eyeball with him in the rear-view mirror. Cobbold was in a nasty position, ve-ry delicate, as he had put it to Kipper. 'It's the Salvation Syndrome,' Cobbold had said, 'which is a shame and an abomination when it strikes at the single man – usually women though, hadn't you noticed? – but the very devil when it gets going in a family. Personally, I think Mad Jack has the hots for Sister Veal and is sublimating his passion because Mrs Mad Jack wouldn't like it. So where does Cobbold come in? you are asking yourself.'

'So where do you come in?' Kipper asked. They had been loitering in the cycle shed.

'I'm a good excuse for them to meet each other, Mad Jack being my brother's brother-in-law and Sister V. my mother's cousin, and between them they're going to save my soul.'

'I don't know what the hell you're on about,' Kipper said.

'Exactly that: Hell. Do you want to hear a really good joke?' said Cobbold, very bitter among the bicycles. 'I'm going to be redeemed.'

'I'm damned if I'd be redeemed,' Kipper said. 'Why don't you just say no?'

'We do as we're told in our house,' Cobbold said. 'It's the dreaded old syndrome again. There's Mum collecting for missionaries and Dad running the Sunday School like it was the SAS. Crack troops for God. He has me out there at the front reading sponge-cake Bible stories and operating the flannelgraph. He doesn't know what I do with that flannelgraph. People in flannelgraphs,' said Cobbold, 'can be put in any position. But *any* position. So up comes Mad Jack and says there's this great preacher touring the collieries. Why doesn't young Tim come along and hear him? An experience he'd never forget. If he's so great, I ask myself, why is he touring the collieries? Why isn't he packing them in at Wembley Stadium?'

'Why are you telling me all this?'

'Because if I can't get out of going – and I can't get out of going – I'm not going alone. My old mate Kipper's coming along as moral support.'

'Oh no he's not,' Kipper said. 'What d'you need moral support for, anyway? If he's that boring you can just go to sleep for the duration.'

Cobbold made small hissing sounds of impatience.

'I told you, they're not taking me along to listen, they're taking me to be saved. It isn't the first time, and if they don't hit the jackpot with this one there'll be another, and more after that. Dad wants me baptized and we have to hear the Call first. I told him I'd be baptized if that was what he wanted, but he said no, I have to wait for God's Call. It doesn't matter what *he* wants, and it doesn't matter what *I* want; just what God wants, and when He wants me, He'll call.'

'Suppose He doesn't want you?'

'Oh, He'll want me. Dad's been on at Him for years.'

'You don't believe in all that?' Kipper said, watching Cobbold's angry and unpractised blush.

'No, but I'm afraid they'll wear me down. In the end I'll just give in, and then it's down into the pit with young Tim.'

'What pit? I thought –'

'That bit of floor with a big trap door, in front of the pulpit. They lift that up and there's a damn great bath underneath. And along comes Pastor Atkinson in his Geneva bands and gum boots, and down I go. Total immersion.'

'Christ!'

'He'll be there,' Cobbold said. 'So do us a favour, eh, Kip? Moral support? Next Sunday?'

Kipper and Cobbold stood in the Cobbolds' embalmed front room and waited for Mr Jack and Miss Veal to come

and collect them in the car. Mr and Mrs Cobbold spoke of
the car as if it were unique, as if, like the phoenix, there
could never be more than one car at a time. When the car
drew up at the gate it turned out to be a green Morris
Minor, aggressively dated, and no less aggressively dated
was Miss Veal, who waited on the pavement while Mr
Jack bounded up to the front door, finger extended eagerly
to meet the bell push. She was wearing a floral print dress
that carefully denied its own shape and hers, and her hair
was as carefully unstyled. Someone had worked hard to
suppress any sign of natural growth while at the same time
avoiding artifice. On her feet tan kayaks, with heels that
seemed to stick out as far behind as the toes did in front,
modestly disguised any hint of an instep, implying that
feet were indelicate. Kipper noted with shock that in spite
of all this she was pretty, with the unused face of a young
girl, only he could see, by the way she stood, that she was
not a young girl. Her leather shoulder bag looked like a
school satchel.

Now she sat before him in the passenger seat, bland as a
blancmange, beside Mr Jack the driver. Her pronounce-
ment on God's personal prejudices had been the only words
spoken since the journey began, except for occasional, and
identical, inquiries from Mr Jack: 'Everyone all right thah,
at the back?' as though Kipper and Cobbold might have
come to some harm, or escaped.

Kipper closed his eyes on the soft evening outside, where
late roses scented the air, and pretended that it was snow-

ing, imagined a creeping cold, visualized his fingers turning blue and his breath freezing upon the air before him, so that he might better savour the surprise when he opened his eyes again on September. Almost he heard wolves howling.

'Whah ah we gahng, e'zzatly?' Cobbold asked, in an indiscreet imitation of Mr Jack's yawning tones.

'Baahthaahn,' said Mr Jack. 'Beyond Cantabrah.'

'Ah,' Cobbold said, lowering his head until his mouth was below the scope of the mirror. 'Berethorne,' he translated, out of the side of closed lips. 'Beyond Canterbury.'

'Zah Chah,' said Mr Jack.

'Zoar Chapel,' Cobbold said.

'Brah Hah is a very moving speakah.'

'Brother Hann is a very moving speaker.'

'Just back from Onk Onk.'

'*Where?*' Cobbold said.

'Onk Onk. Next to China,' Mr Jack said.

'Hong Kong,' Kipper murmured.

'Where the nuts come from,' Cobbold said.

After this Kipper began to notice the extraordinary number of chapels that flourished by the roadside: in the bigger villages gaunt rendered classical temples, sejant, with their front paws on the pavement; in the country tin sheds, asbestos sheds, weatherboard sheds, half-timbered pre-fabs like fifteenth-century garages crouched in little groves of bushes as if something in the soil favoured their development, or reared stark out of bare hillsides like granite outcrops that had resisted erosion. Above the car's engine he sometimes heard the tremulous groan of a harmonium.

'Throbbing organ,' he whispered to Cobbold. Cobbold half-smiled.

He was still thinking of snow when they arrived at Bere-thorne, and it was still light, so that he could see only too clearly what the snow might have concealed. He spread snow with a generous eye over the slagheaps, the small unKentish cottages in their tight-fitting gardens, but leaving the winding gear in dark silhouette, as it would have been in a painting of industrial realism. The Berethorne chapel, constructed out of old railway sleepers and painted a dull, villainous red, stood at the end of a cinder path among allotments where threadbare turf paths divided rectangles of bolted cabbages and, at the intersections, like little slagheaps, stood piles of soot. Kipper had expected to scent coal in the air, but all he could smell was soot. Cobbold lingered on the cinder path, face to face at last with the Red Widow, his foot on the steps to the scaffold and unable to turn back.

A notice tacked to the fence announced that Brother John Hann would speak there at seven o'clock, God willing.

'Maybe He's not willing,' Cobbold suggested, in an undertone. 'Maybe He has caused a subsidence, and the ground has opened up under Brother Hann. Mother Kent's moving.'

'Who?'

'That's what they say in the mines,' said Cobbold, 'when the roof caves in.'

Behind them, Miss Veal's kayaks beached themselves on the cinder path.

'The dah is at the side,' Mr Jack observed, pointing to where the path skirted the corner of the chapel and led them to a curiously fretworked porch, like a sliver pared from a Swiss chalet and grafted on to the chapel in the hope that it would improve the stock. Kipper thought it looked reassuringly frivolous as they went inside.

'Lasciate ogni speranza voi ch'entrate.' Cobbold again, a mocking imp at his ear hole.

'Eh?'

'All hope abandon,' Cobbold said as they followed Mr Jack and Miss Veal into the ill-lit interior, 'ye who enter here.'

The interior was not at all frivolous nor, on the other hand, even slightly religious. It reminded Kipper of the Labour Party Headquarters over Gibbs Furniture Showroom; bare boards, distempered walls, scabrous ceiling; utility blasted by disuse. On either side three mean windows admitted the waning daylight between old red curtains. Old red hassocks sprouted from the floor like leaf galls. Between the rows of pews ran a length of old red carpet and an old red cloth draped a table that stood on a platform at the front of the hall. The fabric looked fibrous and rusty, chafing the eye, raising a prickly rash in armpit and groin. The air tasted of cold dust.

Limp hymnbooks were dealt into their hands by a man in a loose grey suit, and Mr Jack led his party into a pew halfway down the hall, on the right; not too eagerly near the front, not too casually near the back; decently distanced. Next to Mr Jack was Miss Veal, already kneeling on a hassock, head bent, then Cobbold, neck extended to meet the descending blade, and Kipper on the end. Kipper assumed a praying posture which allowed him to survey the scene from beneath a pious hand, without seeming to do so. Over the hunched shoulder of a solitary worshipper in the next pew he saw that on the platform, in front of the red-shrouded table, stood a tripod with a microphone clipped to its neck; its tubular aluminium struts shone incongruously in the murk. He glanced over his shoulder, and again towards the table. The auditorium could not be more than forty feet from front to back; why a microphone at all? He looked sideways. Cobbold had fallen victim to rigor mortis; his frozen profile pointed due east, towards the table. Behind them two women whispered together. He eavesdropped on their devotions.

'My sister's first was born with a caul,' said one. 'They asked the nurse for it, but she said no, she was going to sell it to a sailor. She said they always took cauls and sold them to sailors.'

'We kept Tony's and mounted it on a postcard.' There was a long pause. Kipper, who did not know what a caul was, but who felt that there was something intrinsically naughty in selling things to sailors, endured horrid conjectures. 'But then Tony *is* a sailor,' said Tony's mother. Kipper wondered if Tony who kept his caul on a postcard was among the congregation, and looked right round. The two women were alone in their pew, and behind them two others, with a single man at the end of the bench. He counted ten pews on either side of the hall, and his own, with the four of them in it, was the most densely populated. At a pinch, he supposed, you could pack in about one hundred and fifty really fervent worshippers on the pine benches, with perhaps another fifty standing at the back and rolling in the aisle. So far there were twenty-nine persons awaiting redemption with as much animation as they might have waited for an interview in the Social Security office, while others quietly filtered in through the side door to be welcomed with hymnbooks. There were no greetings, no physical contact. No one shook hands; even those sitting established a careful distance one from another. The man with the hymnbooks smiled as he doled them out, but it was the only smile in the room, discounting Cobbold's grimlie rictus. If this were a revival meeting, they certainly needed reviving.

'People ah coming from all ahvah Kent, I b'lahve,' Mr Jack remarked, as if believing could make it so.

'Praise God,' murmured Miss Veal, with overweening simplicity.

When Kipper had counted forty-one men and women

distributed in accidental quincunxes throughout the hall, the door closed with an unforgiving thud. The man with the hymnbooks deposited those remaining on a bamboo table and sank gracelessly on to a bench. Another grey-suited man descended upon the harmonium and dropped his hands over the keys. A third man in a grey suit climbed on to the platform, knocked over the microphone – which clumsiness earned him not even a smirk – picked it up, and cried, 'Brothers and Sisters, we will sing a hymn of redemption.' The microphone was not switched on.

The Brothers and Sisters rose languidly to their feet. Kipper mouthed words of redemption to a tune that he did not know while Cobbold, mute at his side, began to look more and more like Queen Christina, leaving Sweden forever by boat. Leaden voices all round fell short of the note and plopped to the floor. Kipper recalled the much jollier *ambiance* of his great-grandma's funeral which had been positively effervescent with old ladies all congratulating each other, and themselves, on not being the deceased.

During the last verse the door behind the table opened and another man stepped out. He wore a grey lounge suit and beamed with the murderous bonhomie of a Soviet politician. Kipper knew at once that this must be Brother Hann, although his appearance was met with stunning indifference by the congregation who were baying Amen and in the process of reseating themselves. A fifth man in a grey suit rose from a lair behind the harmonium, stretched out his hand towards the table and proclaimed, 'Brother John Hann.'

'From Onk Onk,' muttered Cobbold, subsiding into a pensive pose with elbow on knee and forehead on fist: Rodin's *Thinker*. An over-enthusiastic handmaid at the back said morosely, 'Praise God,' and Brother Hann, smiling, switched on the microphone to address his flock.

'Let us pray,' he said.

The din was frightful. Brother Hann, travelling with his own audio system, was projected to the faithful of Berethorne in quadraphonic sound. From all corners of the tiny hall his four loudspeakers heckled and exhorted each other to come before the Throne, in a violent Canadian accent that roared from a gulf between Brother Hann's fat lips. The lips were barely an inch from the microphone, but it was a different instrument that Brother Hann had in mind.

'How many of you,' he demanded, 'have a telephone?' He did not stay for an answer. 'We call the telephone a modern miracle of communication. It brings the absent close, friends and loved ones can speak to each other across vast distances.' His arms described vast distances. 'But!' his voice dropped, mercifully, 'how often does this so-called miracle *fail* us? Don't we all know the disappointment when we lift the receiver and dial the number –' his finger shot out. He dialled – 'and NO ONE ANSWERS! What do we say then, Brothers and Sisters? What do we say when the line is engaged, or the number is unobtainable? We say, "This is no miracle." But, Friends, there is a miracle that never fails. I can tell you of a telephone that never goes unanswered. PRAYER!' he shouted, 'is the Hot Line to God. When you pick up that receiver, Brothers and Sisters, God answers every time. That is one line that is never engaged. That line is never *down*. God's number is never unobtainable. He is never ex-directory; and it costs you NOTHING! You can call him collect – reverse the charges,' he translated, for the Old World monoglots. 'God is *in*. He is standing at that great switchboard, longing for you to call. Friends, call him now. He is waiting to hear those telephones ring. In my Father's house there are many mansions, and there's an extension in *every room*!'

The Brothers and Sisters flopped on to their hassocks like broody hens.

'Brothers and Sisters, pray! Dial that number and pray. In Heaven those bells are ringing!'

Kipper's own hassock split as his knees hit it. Something black spilled out. He looked down through his fingers thinking that the thrifty miners had stuffed it with coal dust, or possibly soot. Sonorous breathing all round confirmed that the Brothers and Sisters had made their connection.

Brother Hann, batteries recharged, rose up again. 'He is listening now,' he declared, the head of the microphone almost in his mouth. 'Didn't I tell you? Every time that bell rings, he picks up that hand set.' To Kipper's acute discomfort, Brother Hann then gave a spirited impression of a telephone bell. 'He never lets a call go unanswered.

Mind you,' Brother Hann said, brutally revealing the worm in the apple, 'that answer may be no!'

Kipper looked round. He could not imagine any of the Berethorne congregation using a telephone. It would be too exciting. A call might take years off their lives. They had all too clearly the look of people who knew quite well that the answer was going to be no, and would save themselves from disappointment by declining to ask in the first place. On the other hand, he suddenly had a very clear picture of St Peter standing on a cloud with a receiver held away from his ear, one palm laid discreetly over the mouthpiece.

'Brother Hann on the line, Sir.'

God cringed.

'Tell him I'm out, for God's sake.'

He poked a finger into the hassock's ebon stuffing. It seemed to be asphalt.

One by one the congregation, as if in response to a time signal, replaced their receivers and climbed back into their pews. Brother Hann proposed a hymn; no one argued. Brother Hann drank a mighty glass of water and took up the microphone again. Kipper was pleased to see that he had neglected to switch it on.

'Friends,' said Brother Hann, 'Brothers and Sisters, I am going to tell you a story. I am going to tell you the story of the Prodigal Son. I know – I know –' he held out a tempest-quelling hand over his inert audience, '– you've heard it before. You've heard it many times. I've heard it many times. But tonight, Friends, let us hear it with a new voice. Let it speak to us, every one, in his own heart and, who knows –?' here he switched on the microphone again, '– IT MAY TOUCH THE HEART OF A STRAYING SHEEP. EVEN SILENCE CAN SPEAK TO THE EAR THAT WANTS TO HEAR.'

Kipper looked at Cobbold. Cobbold, the lost sheep, was huddled in a heap of anguished repentance, forehead almost touching the back of the pew in front. Across his shoulders Kipper saw Miss Veal, chin tilted in expectation of ecstasy. A pulse jumped in her neck.

Brother Hann's rendering of the Prodigal Son was unexceptionable, if damaging to the inner ear. He stood foursquare, bisected by the vertical tripod, to speak in a measured manner, and in the words of St Luke.

'A certain man had two sons. And the younger of them said to his father, Father, give me the portion of goods that falleth to me. And he divided unto them his living. And not many days after the younger son gathered all together, and took his journey into a far country, and there wasted his substance with riotous living.'

'Gimme, oh gimme, some of that riotous living,' yearned an envious voice at Kipper's right knee.

'And when he had spent all, there rose a mighty famine in that land, and he began to be in want. And he went and joined himself to a citizen of that country, and he sent him into his fields to feed swine. And he would fain have filled his belly with the husks that the swine did eat: and no man gave unto him. And when he came to himself,' here Brother Hann went down in a thunderous genuflexion, faithfully recorded and relayed by his sound system, unhooked the microphone and hectored it with meaty passion that turned him the colour of fresh liver, 'he said, How many servants of my father's have bread enough and to spare, and I perish with hunger!'

Brother Hann's eyeballs rolled upward. His build was not suggestive of famine.

'I will arise and go to my father and say unto him, Father, I have sinned against heaven and before thee. And am no more worthy to be called thy son: make me as one of thy hired servants.

'And he arose.' Brother Hann arose. Clutching his forehead and limping badly, he looked his last upon the swine and began to walk to and fro across the platform. The trailing cable snaked beside him and described dangerous loops about his feet. After perhaps the fifth crossing he halted, raised his hand to shade his eyes, and stared into the distance.

'But when he was yet a great way off, his father saw him, he *saw* him, and had compassion, Brothers and Sisters he had *compassion*, and ran, and fell on his neck and kissed him.'

Brother Hann broke into a run, his arms spread wide. At the end of the platform he turned and ran back. He was superb. He met himself in the middle, fell on his neck and kissed him.

The father, bosom heaving, withdrew to wipe away a tear. The son, down on one knee again, groaned aloud.

'Father, I have sinned against heaven and in thy sight and am no more worthy to be called thy son. I am unworthy, Father, Father, I am unworthy. I have sinned, I have erred, I have strayed . . . debauched . . . fornicated . . .' Hann swayed back and forth on his considerable haunches, the microphone gripped helplessly between his clenched hands. 'Father forgive me. I am dirt under your feet. I am scum. I am filth!' Flecks appeared at the edges of his mouth, spittle flew, and the relentless screaming boomeranged back at him from the four loudspeakers. Under the onslaught he grovelled, knees and elbows on the scarifying red drugget. 'Father forgive me,' the dreadful voice insisted. 'I should be spat on, spurned, cast into a pit of filth, I am soiled, defiled in thy sight, we are all soiled – '

Crimson as the carpet he rocked and rolled and wrestled with the microphone like a bloated infant Herakles strangling a serpent. Kipper, repelled beyond laughter by the writhing, yelling, spitting, looked first at his hassock, then at the Brothers and Sisters. Impassively, eyes front, they sat in their pews. Cobbold, in such company, had nothing to fear.

The screaming stopped. Brother Hann scrambled to his feet and replaced the microphone. Sweat that had sprung from his engorged face spotted the lapels of his grey suit. He bowed his head and said hoarsely, 'And his father forgave him.

'Now let us pray,' he said, in a still small voice. There was no more talk of telephones. 'Let us pray that through the word of God, Brothers and Sisters, through God's word, yes Friends, that was God's word, some prodigal sons and daughters have been called to redemption. Let us think on the words we have heard, and those of us who have heard the Call, can raise our hands.'

One of the lounge suits began to grind a meandering tuneless moan from the harmonium as the congregation settled onto its hassocks. Kipper looked about him for the raised hands. The music died. Cobbold's hands were clenched on the back of the next pew, as though he could not trust them to lie idle. The silence became oppressive, then embarrassing. Surely someone . . .

Kipper closed his eyes and rehearsed Brother Hann's contortions. Brother Hann was now on his knees again, behind the table. The Brothers and Sisters knelt on, elbows clamped firmly to their sides, hands clasped. Suppose no one . . . Would they have to stay there until somebody . . . Like at school, when the malefactor wouldn't own up. The harmonium resumed its fitful wheezing, like a stomach rumbling in an empty room. They would be there all night. Brother Hann was waiting. Oh, please God, let one of these lumps be moved to feel something. After all that . . . *that* . . . He felt an arm raised. It was his own.

He must surely have imagined the great gust of relief that ventilated the hall, but it was a real, furious voice in his ear that said, 'What the *hell* did you do that for?'

He shielded his face with his forearm and said, 'Someone had to. Now we can all go home.'

'Go home? Do you think they've finished with you?' He had never heard Cobbold sound so haggard. His voice was sick with anger. 'They'll never let me alone now. You've done it this time, you *bloody* fool, you've really done it . . .'

'I had to. I couldn't stand any more.'

'Couldn't stand any more? My God, you haven't even started.'

Stiffly they all climbed to their feet to sing a final hymn, and down the aisle came Brother Hann, to claim his prodigal.

'*You haven't even started*,' Cobbold repeated savagely, as Kipper was led away by the lounge suits to be saved in public, on the platform, and he knew too late why Cobbold had blushed in the bicycle shed, and why Cobbold's face was now so white with wintry rage.

Other titles in *Plus*

High Pavement Blues *Bernard Ashley*
Easy Connections *Liz Berry*
Ganesh *Malcolm J. Bosse*
Empty World *John Christopher*
The Village by the Sea *Anita Desai*
The Seventh Raven *Peter Dickinson*
The Summer After the Funeral *Jane Gardam*
Summer of My German Soldier *Bette Greene*
The Endless Steppe *Esther Hautzig*
Buddy *Nigel Hinton*
The Ennead *Jan Mark*
Jacob Have I Loved *Katherine Paterson*
Flambards Divided *K. M. Peyton*
Sweet Frannie *Susan Sallis*
The Scarecrows *Robert Westall*
Break of Dark *Robert Westall*